Where the rain come from?

Sheriff Joe Mountain glanced at the woman on the seat beside him. She didn't need to be conscious to tell him something had happened out there. He might not have lived on the reservation in years, but there was enough Navaho left in him to know something was out of harmony.

Wandering around in rainy weather like this, she had to be half-frozen. Joe reached across the seat, running the backs of his fingers along her cheek. Even against his cold hands, her skin felt like ice. Yet frigid skin and drenched hair couldn't hide her delicate features. She was a beautiful woman.

How had she ended up in a place like this? The fear he'd seen in her eyes before she'd collapsed was something he would never forget.

"What's got you so frightened, rain lady? What can I do to help you?"

Dear Reader,

Valentine's Day is here this month, and what better way to celebrate the spirit of romance than with six fabulous novels from Silhouette Intimate Moments? Kathleen Creighton's *The Awakening of Dr. Brown* is one of those emotional tours de force that will stay in your mind and your heart long after you've turned the last page. With talent like this, it's no wonder Kathleen has won so many awards for her writing. Join Ethan Brown and Joanna Dunn on their journey into the heart. You'll be glad you did.

A YEAR OF LOVING DANGEROUSLY continues with *Someone To Watch Over Her,* a suspenseful and sensuous Caribbean adventure by Margaret Watson. Award winner Marie Ferrarella adds another installment to her CHILDFINDERS, INC. miniseries with *A Hero in Her Eyes,* a real page-turner of a romance. Meet the second of bestselling author Ruth Langan's THE SULLIVAN SISTERS in *Loving Lizbeth*—and look forward to third sister Celeste's appearance next month. Reader favorite Rebecca Daniels is finally back with *Rain Dance,* a gripping amnesia story. And finally, check out *Renegade Father* by RaeAnne Thayne, the stirring tale of an irresistible Native American hero and a lady rancher.

All six of this month's books are guaranteed to keep you turning pages long into the night, so don't miss a single one. And be sure to come back next month for more of the best and most exciting romantic reading around—right here in Silhouette Intimate Moments.

Enjoy!

Leslie J. Wainger
Executive Senior Editor

Please address questions and book requests to:
Silhouette Reader Service
U.S.: 3010 Walden Ave., P.O. Box 1325, Buffalo, NY 14269
Canadian: P.O. Box 609, Fort Erie, Ont. L2A 5X3

Rain Dance
REBECCA DANIELS

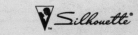

INTIMATE MOMENTS™

Published by Silhouette Books

America's Publisher of Contemporary Romance

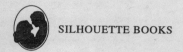 SILHOUETTE BOOKS

ISBN 0-373-27131-X

RAIN DANCE

Copyright © 2001 by Ann Marie Fattarsi

Visit Silhouette at www.eHarlequin.com

Printed in U.S.A.

REBECCA DANIELS

will never forget the first time she read a Silhouette novel. "I was at my sister's house, sitting by the pool and trying without much success to get interested in the book I'd brought from home. Everything seemed to distract me—the dog, the kids, the seagulls. Finally my sister plucked the book from my hands, told me she was going to give me something I wouldn't be able to put down and handed me my first Silhouette novel. Guess what? She was right! For that lazy afternoon by her pool, I will forever be grateful." From that day on, Rebecca has been writing romance novels and loving every minute of it.

Born in the Midwest but raised in Southern California, she now resides in the scenic coastal community of Santa Barbara with her two sons. She loves early morning walks along the beach, bicycling, hiking, an occasional round of golf and hearing from her fans. You can write to Rebecca in care of Silhouette Books, 300 East 42nd St., New York, NY 10017.

TYVMFE!—and for the morning crew at Goleta Beach:
the doctor, Richard K., Stony, the car salesman,
and the boys on the pier—from the girls.
Anyone for coffee?

Chapter 1

Mesa County Sheriff Joe Mountain slammed down hard on the brakes, locking all four tires on the sturdy four-wheel-drive Jeep vehicle and causing it to careen across the wet pavement to a violent stop. His heart pounded in his chest, reverberating in his ears to blend with the frantic rhythm of the wipers as they furiously moved back and forth across the windshield.

"What the hell?" he murmured aloud, leaning forward in the seat. The wind howled, catching the rain and sending it sheeting across the glass in giant waves. He squinted, trying to make out the image coming toward him on the pavement, but his vision was too blurred, too distorted despite the wipers' best efforts to clear it.

A wounded animal, he thought, rubbing at the inside of the window with the sleeve of his jacket. A coyote maybe, or a mountain lion—or maybe several of them, judging from the size. His gaze narrowed farther, straining to see. A healthy animal would have taken shelter in higher ground long ago.

His hand automatically reached for a switch, bringing the patrol lights alive on the roof of the car, then for the leather strap of the shotgun holster mounted on the dash of the Jeep. Approaching a wounded animal would be too dangerous, even if he did just want to help it, but a couple of shots fired into the air might frighten it off the road. On the highway it posed a hazard and could cause an accident—like the deadly accident he'd just finished investigating and had brought him out to this desolate part of the county in the first place.

But the hand on the holster strap suddenly froze as the moving figure began to take shape and form—and the form it took wasn't that of a coyote. The figure emerging out of the darkness of the storm and into the glow of his headlights was decidedly human, and decidedly female.

A woman.

She couldn't stop shivering, even though she'd stopped feeling her arms and legs long ago. Rendered numb by the bitter wind and rain, she was only vaguely aware of the cold now, and yet she trembled. The fear was still there, still lurking in the blackness that had existed for her before the rain.

She had no idea how long she'd been walking, but it had been long enough to crush the initial panic— panic that had sent her running aimlessly through the desert and screaming at the top of her lungs. At the moment she was more concerned about finding someplace dry, someplace safe, than trying to figure out what had happened and why.

She wouldn't call it a nightmare; it was far worse than that. It felt more like something out of a dark, depressing novel, something existential and surreal and completely without cause—only if it was, she couldn't remember now. All she knew for certain was she was alive—she had to be. If death was a void, this was too terrifying for that.

There was nothing empty, nothing vacant in the place she found herself. It was filled with harsh, brutal feelings and cold, unyielding reality. It was more a displacement of her life than a dissolution. She had opened her eyes to a time and a place she didn't recognize, to a world she didn't know.

"Stranger in a strange land," she muttered aloud, the harsh wind catching her words and sending them flying. She stopped walking, something flickering in her brain. There was something vaguely familiar about the phrase, something almost recognizable—the first recognizable thing she'd found in this terrible place. But it was vague, and there only for a moment. Soon the familiarity was gone, blown from her memory like words on the wind.

She started walking again, and trembling. Where was she? How did she get there, and when could she leave? Why could she remember nothing, and what had been there before the void and the blackness?

Where had she been before she'd been here?

She glanced down at the corduroy blazer and slacks she had on. They were soaked through, and clung to her exhausted body like a second skin. She felt no ownership, no connection to them. They looked alien and unfamiliar to her, just like this barren world around her.

When the lights first appeared over the horizon, her

initial instinct had been to run, to hide, but she fought the fear. Darkness was falling fast, and the thought of being alone in a world of blackness was more terrifying than those small, ominous lights moving over the horizon like eyes of the monster seeking her out.

"Stop," she said, the word taking more energy than she'd expected. Suddenly she was running, running toward the light, her deadened arms waving above her. "Please. Please stop."

Joe stepped out of the car, one hand carefully hovering over the holstered gun inside his jacket.

"Stop right there, ma'am. Don't move."

"Please," she said, staggering a few steps forward. "Please...please help me."

"I said stop," he demanded, raising a hand up. "Don't come any closer."

But she did come closer, stumbling and weaving, her footsteps growing more erratic, more uneven the nearer she got.

"Oh, please," she pleaded again, ignoring his orders. "Help me. Please help—"

She fell forward, lunging toward him with both arms outstretched. Reflex had him diving forward, had him reaching for her. Procedure would have been to let her fall, would have been not to drop his guard until he'd assessed the situation completely—and this whole thing had the earmarks of a setup. She could have lured him to stop, could have a band of cohorts hiding out of sight, ready to swoop down and jump him the moment his back was turned. Only...for some reason, he had been unable to let her fall. For the first time in his professional life, Joe Mountain forgot about procedure, forgot about suspicion and precaution—and he forgot about the gun in his holster. There had been something in her cry for help, something that couldn't be faked or fabricated and the look on her face had told him all he'd needed to know. This was no setup, no highway crime in progress. She wasn't lying in wait, she was terrified and he had to help.

Reaching out, he caught her in his arms, carefully lowering her to the pavement and pillowing her head in his arms. Rain and wind pelted them and he shielded her as best he could.

"Ma'am, can you hear?" He felt for a pulse in her neck and at her wrist. "Wake up. Can you hear me?"

She gave no response, but he could feel the soft, steady throb of a pulse beneath her chin.

He glanced up, looking for signs of a disabled vehicle—skid marks, spilled oil, highway debris, a suitcase, a purse—anything that might explain what had happened to her, but there was nothing.

"Ma'am," he said again, looking back down at her and giving her cheek a tap with the palm of his hand. "Can you hear me?"

Her clothes were drenched, and her long hair streaked down her face. She looked as though she'd been wandering around out there for a while. Running a hand inside her jacket, and around the pockets of her slacks, he felt for evidence of a wallet, of car keys, but her pockets were empty.

"Ma'am, wake up. I'm a police officer, I'm going to get you to a hospital. You're going to be okay." He cupped her chin in his palm and gave her head a small shake. "Can you hear me?"

She breathed out a groan, and her head fell to one side. Then suddenly, with no other warning, her eyes popped open and her head sprang up.

"Logan, no," she screamed, clutching at his jacket. "No, Logan, Loga—"

"L-Logan?" Joe stammered, overwhelmed by the sudden outburst.

But she didn't answer him. With her head falling back, she slipped into unconsciousness again.

"Ma'am?" Joe said, giving her a small shake. "Ma'am?"

Only, there was no reaction this time. A sudden bolt from the clouds sent a brilliant flash of white light over everything, and a thunderous roar from the sky above.

Gathering her up into his arms, Joe carried her to the passenger side of his vehicle, carefully lowering her into the front seat. Securing the seat belt around her, he closed the door tightly.

Stepping away from the car, he took a moment to scan the area. But with the wind whipping at the rain and sending it stinging into his eyes, it was impossible to see more than a few feet. Turning, he made his way back around the car, and climbed inside.

"Base station, this is mobile one, do you read me?" he said, flipping on the radio and looking at the woman slumped against the back of the seat beside him. "Ryan, come on, answer damn it. Do you read me?"

He waited a few anxious seconds for his deputy to respond, the water dripping from the brim of his hat making a small pool on the seat. The storm had made the radio useless all day, but he had to try, had to make an effort.

"Base station, this is mobile one, do you copy?" he said, his impatience growing. "Work, you stupid thing," he growled, giving the radio a slam with the flat of his hand. "Work!" But there was only static on the line, making him all the more furious. "Piece of sh—'' He slammed the microphone down, flipping the radio off and shifting the car into gear.

The thick tires of the Jeep squealed loudly against the wet blacktop as he put the pedal to the metal and started down the highway. Glancing at the woman beside him, he swore under his breath.

Where the hell had she come from? What was she doing out here in the middle of nowhere? He needed to investigate, to look around and try to figure out what had happened, but that required time and decent weather—neither of which he had at the moment. What he did have was a useless radio, and an unconscious woman who needed immediate medical attention and about sixty miles of highway between them and the hospital.

As the Jeep picked up speed, he flipped on his siren and glanced out the windows at the nearly dark countryside. It had been a cold, miserable day—starting at dawn with the report of a five-car pileup along the Nevada-Utah border.

Given the choice, he would have liked nothing more than to have weathered the miserable storm holed up in his office—warm and dry and comfortable. But this was Mesa County—his county—and that meant he didn't have a choice. When something happened in this rugged, remote corner of the state, Sheriff Joe Mountain wanted to know all about it.

He glanced back to the woman on the seat beside him. She didn't need to be conscious to tell him something had definitely happened out here, something pretty unusual. He may not have lived on the reservation in years, but there was enough Navajo left in him to know something was out of harmony, out of balance. In the dim light of the dashboard, her lips looked blue with cold and her skin was an ashen white. No wonder she'd collapsed. Wandering around in weather like this, she had to be half-frozen.

Wedging his knee against the steering wheel, he shrugged out of his jacket. The buckskin leather was soaked, but the white, wooly lining was warm and dry. With one hand, he covered her with the coat, tucking it around her tight.

Looking at her, he felt something tighten in his chest. This whole thing had him feeling restless and unsettled. Things didn't fit; *she* didn't fit. She didn't belong here, wasn't dressed for rough weather and rough country. She looked more like she belonged in a trendy coffeehouse somewhere sipping caffe lattes, or shopping in some stylish boutique.

He reached across the seat, running the backs of his fingers along her cheek. Even against his cold hands, her skin felt like ice. Yet frigid skin and drenched hair couldn't hide her delicate features. He might be a cop investigating a possible accident or potential crime, but he was also a man, and he would have had to be dead not to notice just how lovely she was. She was a beautiful woman—a very beautiful woman. She had an almost perfect face—delicate, refined, feminine—which only added to his uneasiness. How did someone like her end up in a place like this?

Reaching down, he adjusted the heater vents, directing them toward her, and let his foot press down harder on the gas. Looking through the windshield at the road ahead, he shifted uneasily against the seat. He'd been a law enforcement officer for nearly fifteen years, and he'd seen a lot in that time—tragic accidents, grisly crime scenes. But the fear he had seen in her eyes that moment before she'd collapsed was something he would never forget.

"What's got you so frightened, rain lady? Is it Logan?" he said, reaching across the seat and running a finger down her cheek again. "Is Logan what sent you running into my county?"

"So what do you think, Doc?"

"I don't know," Cruz Martinez mumbled, letting the eyelid of the woman on the gurney gently close and flipping the tiny beam of his penlight off.

"What do you mean, you don't know?" Joe insisted, stepping to one side to let two paramedics push past him. "You're a doctor, you should be able to tell something."

"You're right, I'm a doctor, not a fortune-teller," Cruz said, straightening up. He reached for the end of the gurney and pushed it toward the doors of Mesa County General's ER. "Joe, come on, give me a break. The woman just got here."

"Okay, all right, okay," he conceded, grabbing the other side of the gurney and helping him push it through the doors and into the crowded emergency room. "But she'll be all right, won't she? You think she's going to be okay, don't you—"

"Joe," Cruz said, cutting him off. He gestured to one of the nurses, who rushed to assist him. "Give me a few minutes, let me see what we've got here and then I'll let you know."

"Sure, sure, okay," Joe said, following the gurney past the nurses' desk and through the swinging doors to the examination rooms. "But—"

"Joe," Cruz said in a calm voice, stopping him at the entrance of the examination room. "Let me do my job.'' He reached up, catching hold of the curtain and giving it a yank. ''So then you can do yours.''

''Right,'' Joe said with a resigned sigh as Cruz slid the curtain closed between them. ''I'll, uh, just be outside,'' he said to no one in particular.

Turning around, he slowly made his way back through the swinging doors and to the long row of chairs in the emergency waiting room. Sitting down, he slipped off his damp cowboy hat and rubbed at his tired, scratchy eyes.

He knew he was being unreasonable, knew he had to be patient and just cool his heels until Cruz had a chance to examine her, he just didn't feel like waiting. He'd been waiting for the last hour it had taken to drive back to Mesa Ridge—an hour the ''rain woman'' had spent unconscious.

Rain Woman. That was how he'd come to think of her—woman of the rain. He lived and worked in the world of the white man, but his mind and his soul were still Navajo, still relating everything to the elemental basics in life—sun, moon, earth, sky, wind and rain. She had come into his world with the rain, so to him she was Rain.

''Rain,'' he muttered, thinking of the woman who was as puzzling, as enigmatic as the elements themselves. It was time to balance the scales, to put the world back in its place again. He'd waited, now he wanted action. He had questions, now he wanted answers. It was time for balance.

''You look like you could use this.''

Joe looked up, surprised to see Cruz Martinez's wife, Marcy, standing in front of him with a foam cup of coffee in her hand. "Marcy, hello. What are you doing here?"

"Well, I was hoping to get my husband out of here at a reasonable hour, but..." She stopped and glanced back at the doors leading to the examination rooms. "You pretty much took care of that."

Joe grimaced apologetically. "Sorry about that."

"I'm getting used to it," Marcy confessed with a resigned sigh, turning back to him and offering him the steaming cup of coffee. "I was just hoping we could have a few hours together this evening since I'll be taking off for the state capital tomorrow."

"Giving up the bench for the governor's office?"

Marcy laughed. "Just hearing a change of venue case up there for a few weeks." She looked down at the cup in her hand. "Here, drink this before it gets cold."

Joe smiled up at her. He'd barely known Marcy when she'd married Cruz two years ago, but since then he'd come to not only like her, but admire her as well. In addition to being a devoted wife and mother, she was also a Mesa County Superior Court Judge.

"Thanks," he said, taking several sips of hot brew, savoring its black, bitter taste.

"Better?"

Joe nodded. "Much."

"If you don't mind me saying so, Sheriff Mountain, you look a little like a drowned rat."

"I don't mind, *Your Honor,*" he admitted. "I happen to feel a little like a drowned rat at the moment."

She gestured back to the examination rooms with a nod of her head. "Accident victim?"

Joe shook his head slowly, glancing at the closed doors, and shook his head. "Got me."

Marcy frowned. "You don't know?"

Joe thought of the woman, thought of Rain and the million scenarios that had raced through his mind when he'd seen her step out of the gloom and into the beam of his headlights. He would have found it less puzzling, less unsettling if she'd done something simple, like pull a gun on him. At least things would have been clear then, cut-and-dried. At least it would have explained what she was doing out there.

"No, I don't," he said after a moment, his gaze slowly moving to Marcy's. "I picked her up out on the highway. She was wandering around out there all by herself."

"In this storm?" Marcy's brow furrowed. "Poor thing. Where was this?"

"Out on Route 16," Joe said, remembering the fear he had seen in her eyes. "About twenty miles south of the Hollister place."

"The Hollister place!" Marcy gasped, her eyes wide with surprise now. "Way up there? What would she be doing wandering around there?"

"Your guess is as good as mine," he said with a tired sigh. The fatigue of a too long day with too little sleep had suddenly begun to take hold. "There was no car, no sign of an accident."

Marcy's frown deepened. "You suspect foul play?"

Joe shrugged. "At this point I'm looking at everything." He slowly stood up, tossing the empty cup into the sand of the ashtray beside the chair. He turned and looked at the closed doors of the examination rooms. "She was unconscious when I brought her in, I'm hoping when she wakes up..." He stopped and glanced back to Marcy. "Well, I'd like to question her when she wakes up."

"Cruz say what he thought was wrong with her?"

Joe thought of that curtain being closed in his face, and scowled. "Cruz didn't *say* anything."

Marcy smiled. "Yes, well, I know how that go— Oh, wait—here he is."

Joe had to stop himself from running across the corridor to meet the doctor at the door.

"Is she okay, Doc?" he asked, surprised by the sound of alarm in his own voice. "Is she awake?"

"She's awake," Cruz said, spotting his wife and steering Joe back into the direction of the waiting area. "But she's very weak." He slipped an arm around Marcy's waist, giving her a kiss on the cheek. Reluctantly, he turned back to Joe, swiping an arm across his forehead. "And she's exhausted."

"But can I talk to her?" Joe asked eagerly.

Cruz turned and looked at him. "I don't think it's going to do much good."

Joe felt something go dead in him. "Why, what's the matter?"

"She doesn't remember."

"What do you mean she doesn't remember?"

"She doesn't remember," Cruz said again. "She doesn't remember anything." He glanced down at Marcy, then back to Joe. "What we have here is a case of amnesia."

Chapter 2

"Good morning, Miss Rain."

The voice came from out of the darkness, sounding bright and sunny and safe. It reached down into the shadows like a hand extending out to her and she felt herself struggling, felt herself reaching. She wanted that hand, wanted up and out of the gloom.

"Rise and shine, it's not raining this morning. Maybe we should call you Sunshine now."

Suddenly her head was filled with sound and shafts of light pierced the layers of her eyelids, obliterating the darkness and sending the nightmare to the back of her brain. Thank God, it had been a dream. It all had been just a terrible dream.

"Come on now, sleepyhead, open up those eyes. Breakfast is being served. We've got to get you fed and down to the lab for a whole pack of tests the doctor has planned for you. Come on now, wake up. I know you wouldn't want to miss any of the fun."

Noise and light assaulted her, making her forget about panic and fear. She welcomed the chaos, welcomed the voice that coaxed her awake. She wanted to open her eyes and have her world made right again.

"What do we have here? Ah yes, oatmeal—nice and lumpy—our kitchen's specialty. Come on now, Miss Rain. Let me see those eyes open."

The light was blinding at first, painful and unyielding against eyes accustomed only to darkness. Still, it felt warm and comforting against her skin. There was a moment when it seemed that her eyes had forgotten how to function, when she could make out nothing of what she saw and the world was reduced to indistinguishable, unrecognizable blurred images. However, slowly those blurry, distorted images came into focus and she found herself looking into a face that looked as kind and as friendly as its voice sounded.

"Atta girl. Let's see those…" The voice drifted off as she leaned in for a closer look. "Looks like there might be some blue in there. Open them up darlin'. Let's get a good look at those baby blues."

Her throat felt raw and coarse and she thought of how small and lost her screams had sounded in the desert.

And then she remembered. She may be waking up, but the nightmare wasn't over—and for a moment, panic put a stranglehold on her throat.

"Wh-where am I?"

"You're in Mesa County General Hospital. Do you remember talking to the doctor last night?"

Jumbled, confused images of people and faces flashed suddenly into her brain and she remembered waking up to noise and confusion. How frightening it had been to wake up and find herself being poked and prodded by strangers, but at least she'd been out of the desert, at least she hadn't been alone.

"He asked questions," she croaked, lifting a hand to her throat. The words hurt. "He gave me a shot."

"Something to help you rest," the woman said. "But there's no time to sleep now. Let's get some food in you and get you down to the lab or Dr. Martinez is going to have my head on a platter."

"I—I don't remember."

"You don't remember? You mean, talking to the doctor?"

She shook her head, pain radiating as dread rose up from her belly like a wave on the shore. "You—you don't understand. I don't remember *anything*."

"When you're ready you will," the woman said breezily, maneuvering the control switch along the bed frame and raising the back of the bed. "And these tests may help."

"Tests?" It was only then that she realized the woman was wearing a nurse's uniform. "They'll help me remember?"

"Well, not the tests themselves," the nurse qualified. "But they'll help the doctor know just what's going on inside that pretty head of yours."

"I—I don't remember how..." she stammered, wincing as her hand brushed the hair along the back of her head. "I don't know how that bump on my head happened, either."

"Try not to think about all that too much right now," the nurse advised. "It's not going to help if you're upset." She propped the pillows. "Now come on, Rain. Eat your breakfast."

She looked down at the food in front of her, the

smell triggering a violent reaction in her stomach. "I—I'm not hungry."

"Too bad," the nurse said with a wry sigh, picking up the spoon and shoving it into her hand. "Hunger usually makes this stuff go down a little easier. Come on now, be a good girl. Dig in."

She looked down at the spoon in her hand and then to the food on the tray. Everything in her system wanted to revolt, wanted to protest the sight and the aroma of the food. It was as if she'd left the nightmare only to awaken into a surreal dream. She was sitting in this strange place looking at food she didn't want and having no idea how she got there. Slowly, she lowered the spoon to the tray and pushed it away.

"You called me something," she said, falling back against the pillows. "Rain? Do you know me? Is that my name?"

The nurse shook her head, sliding the tray back into place. "No, sweetheart, I'm afraid I don't know." She picked up the spoon and scooped it full of oatmeal. "We've been calling you Rain. That's what Sheriff Mountain called you."

"Sheriff Mountain?"

The nurse nodded. "He brought you in last night." She lifted the spoon. "He's the one who found you wandering around out there."

"Sheriff Mountain," she murmured, remembering the headlights of a car, remembering a tall, dark, shadowy figure stepping in front of them and remembering a soft voice and strong arms that felt warm and secure.

"Would you prefer I call you something else?"

She looked up at the nurse. Rain. She liked the name, liked the sound of it. It didn't make her think of the freezing, pelting rain but rather the strong arms that brought her rescue and warmth.

Her name was Rain. Knowing that made her feel better, made her feel less afraid. With a name, she was a real person. With a name, she had something to hold on to.

She squeezed her eyes tight, feeling the panic rise from the depths again. Who was she really? Where did she come from? What had happened to her and why?

"No," she mumbled, opening her eyes. "Rain's fine."

"Okay then, Rain," the nurse coaxed with the spoonful of oatmeal. "Just a little."

Rain looked at the oatmeal and felt her stomach roll. In the long list of things she couldn't remember, she couldn't remember the last time she'd eaten, either. Gingerly, she opened her mouth.

"Good girl," the nurse commended as she watched Rain take a bite. "That doesn't taste too awfully bad, now does it?"

A warm, rich flavor filled her senses and Rain reached for the spoon, shoveling in another mouthful. It was delicious.

"Want me to pour you a glass of milk?" the nurse asked.

Rain nodded, gobbling up another bite. "You said this was Mesa County General Hospital?" The nurse nodded as she poured milk from a small carton and into a glass on the tray. "Where's that?"

"Mesa Ridge. In Nevada," the nurse said, walking to the door and pulling a wheelchair in from the corridor. "Sound familiar?"

Rain took several gulps of milk and shook her head. Reaching for a knife, she spread strawberry preserves over a slice of toast. "Not at all. Is it near Las Vegas? Reno?"

The nurse laughed. "Oh, Rain. Mesa Ridge, Nevada, is about as far away from everything as you can get." Her smile slowly faded. "Which makes me think you're not from around here."

Rain finished the milk and reached for a glass of orange juice. "You don't think so?"

"I don't," the nurse said thoughtfully.

"Why do you say that?"

She shrugged. "I don't know. You just don't look the type."

"I don't?"

A random thought suddenly raced through her brain as she pierced an orange wedge with her fork from the fruit cup on the tray. Did she know what she looked like?

"I don't know. You just look a little too... sophisticated for these parts. We don't get a lot of corduroy blazers and penny loafers out this way. Besides, there may be a lot of land out here, a lot of wide-open spaces, but there aren't that many people so we tend to keep track of one another. Someone from around here turns up missing, you tend to hear about it."

Rain watched as the nurse fussed about her, adjusting the blankets on the bed, fluffing the already fluffed pillows, but her mind was remembering the shadowy figure that had reached for her in the headlights of the car. She remembered how warm and safe she had felt in his arms and longed for that feeling again.

"No one's turned up missing around here?" she asked after a moment.

"Not that I've heard," the nurse admitted. "And

believe me, there isn't much that happens in Mesa
County that I don't know about." She paused for a
moment, then pointed down at the tray. "And I'd say
for someone who isn't hungry, you did a pretty good
job."

Rain glanced down at the dishes, shocked to find
them empty. "I—I had no idea...."

"I don't know that I've ever known anyone to actually finish a bowl of our oatmeal before," the nurse
conceded, pulling a folded hospital robe from a drawer
in the bed stand. "You must have been starvin', darlin'."

Rain had to admit she did feel better. The gnawing
in her stomach had eased and her headache didn't feel
nearly as bad. "I didn't even know I was hungry."

"Maybe not," the nurse said, handing her the robe.
"But your body knew it needed some nutrition." She
pulled the covers on the bed back. "Now put that robe
around you and let's get you going."

Rain looked down at the faded robe, then back up
to the nurse. "Is there a mirror in here?"

The nurse hesitated for a moment, then something
softened in her eyes.

"Right here," she said, flipping back a plastic disk
from a panel beside the bed, revealing a small lighted
mirror on the other side. "And maybe I can scrounge
up a hairbrush, too."

Rain slowly leaned forward, almost reluctant to see
who would look back at her. What if she didn't recognize that face? She was surrounded by a world of
strangers. What if she was a stranger to herself?

"It's...it's me," she whispered, watching the reflection of her own lips move in the mirror. Leaning closer,
she brought a hand to her lips, her cheek, and through

her hair, feeling a wave of relief wash over her. She wasn't sure when the last time was that she had seen the face in the mirror, but it was a familiar face to her—gloriously and gratefully familiar. For the first time since she'd awakened in the desert, she was looking at something familiar.

"This isn't much," the nurse conceded, pulling a small, plastic-wrapped comb from another drawer in the bed stand. "But it might work until we can get you some decent toiletries. Run it through your hair while I get one of the student nurses to take you down to the lab." She glanced down at the oversize watch on her wrist. "X rays aren't scheduled for about an hour but the way those techs in the lab poke around, it'll take them about that long to draw a couple cc's of blood from you."

Rain glanced up, feeling another moment of uneasiness. "You—you won't be coming with me?"

The nurse smiled. "Oh, don't you worry—you haven't seen the last of me yet. We've got a bunch of things planned for you." She helped Rain into the wheelchair and pushed her out of the room and into the corridor where a young woman stood waiting. "This is Terri and she's going to take you for your tests and then in to see Dr. Martinez."

"Will he have the results then?" Rain asked, fear creeping into her voice. What if the doctor's tests reveal that she'd never get better, what if they reveal she never would remember? "When will I know?"

The nurse bent close, covering Rain's hand with hers. There was such kindness in her weathered face, such compassion, Rain couldn't help herself from responding. The woman understood what she was feeling, understood just how frightened she was.

"Don't you worry," she assured Rain in a quiet voice. "We're going to take good care of you, you can be sure of that. And don't forget, there's Sheriff Mountain…he'll figure out what happened out there in the desert, he'll find out where you belong and he'll get you back there—you'll see."

Rain felt a lump of emotion form in her throat and she struggled to swallow. She wanted to believe the nurse, wanted to believe the nightmare could end and that she would find her life again.

"Thank you," she whispered, feeling the sting of tears burn her eyes and her throat.

"And by the way, I'm Carrie," the nurse called after her as Rain was wheeled down the hallway. "If anybody gives you any trouble, you just tell them they'll have me to contend with."

"Was she raped?"

The words slipped out of his mouth as though he were asking about the weather or the score of a ball game. Being Navajo and being a lawman, Joe Mountain had long ago learned the importance of keeping any emotion out of his voice. It never paid to let anyone know how you really felt. It may have played havoc in his private life, but professionally, it was the only way to survive.

Cruz tossed the chart on to his cluttered desktop and drew in a deep breath. Leaning back in his chair, he glanced up at Joe Mountain and shook his head. "I told you—no evidence of sexual assault. No evidence of drugs or alcohol."

Joe made a notation in his notebook and tried to ignore the rush of relief that pulsed through his veins. Acknowledging relief would have been admitting that it mattered and it didn't—it couldn't. As a lawman it was his job to dig out the facts—cold, hard facts. Not react to them.

"Is there a possibility she could have been struck by lightning?"

Cruz snorted at the suggestion and shook his head again. "Lightning strike would cause severe tissue damage—point of entry, point of exit—that sort of thing and there's not a mark on her. No burns, no trauma at least. Just a bump on the head."

Joe made another notation in the tablet. "So that would pretty much leave out an animal attack?"

"Mountain lion, or something like that?"

"Yeah."

"Pretty much," Cruz said with a wry smile. "Not many declawed mountain cats out there. Unless, of course, you meet up with one of those club-carrying cats who prefer whacking their victims over the top of the head." He breathed out a laugh. "You know, caveman style."

Joe glanced up, shooting Cruz a dark look. "No sign of animal attack," he said deliberately, writing as he spoke and enunciating each word carefully.

"Safe to say that," Cruz mumbled, doing his best to look appropriately chastised. They were two men who worked in professions that saw too much human misery and adversity and the dark humor they shared from time to time was a way they helped one another cope. "And just for the record, your lady had no scratch marks on her. No scratches, no scrapes, no bruises—not even a bug bite."

Joe walked to the chair in front of Cruz's desk and sat down. "So you can't come up with any explanation as to what happened to her."

"Not really," Cruz admitted. "The woman sustained a blow to the back of the head which rendered her unconscious. For how long, though, I don't know and whether or not it caused the memory loss she's experiencing, I can't say."

"But you could venture a guess."

Cruz shrugged. "My guess is no—the trauma just doesn't appear to me to be that severe."

"Even though it rendered her unconscious?"

"People get knocked out all the time and they don't lose their memory," Cruz pointed out. "Amnesia is very rare."

Joe tried hard not to let his frustration show in his tone, but it wasn't easy. He wanted answers—needed them in order to put the pieces of the puzzle together, but they just weren't there.

"Serious now," Joe said, himself serious. "What do you think has caused it?"

Cruz's expression changed, all signs of humor gone now. "It's really hard to say," he confessed. "But the fact that the woman has not only forgotten what happened to her, she's forgotten everything else—her name, where she comes from—makes me think whatever it was that happened was so traumatic to her, she's blocked everything out."

"So you think she doesn't want to remember?"

"Not that she doesn't want to remember. More like she can't bring herself to," he explained. "I think whatever happened—whether it was actually something that happened to her or something she witnessed, something she participated in—it was so distressing, so disturbing her mind simply won't let her remember it." Cruz sat up, leaning his elbows on the cluttered desktop. "Now you tell me. What would *you* think happened to the lady?"

Joe flipped his tablet closed and tossed it down on to the desk atop the medical chart. Joe and Cruz had been friends a long time, long enough that Joe felt comfortable sharing ideas and knowing they would go no further.

"Honestly? It beats the hell out of me." Slipping his pencil into the pocket of his shirt, he walked to a chair in front of Cruz's desk and slowly lowered himself into it. "I'm just guessing at this point, trying not to overlook anything—no matter how off the wall it may sound."

"Sort of going on the theory that if you don't have anything to go on," Cruz concluded, "then anything's possible?"

"Something like that," Joe admitted. "At this point I don't know if she's the victim or the perpetrator, if I should be checking out the missing persons lists or the wanted posters, if a crime has been committed or if an accident has happened. Maybe she just ran out of gasoline, or lost control of her car and something snapped, making her forget everything." He rolled his shoulders back, easing hard, tense muscles. "Maybe she fell, or slid down a mountain—hell! She could've dropped from the sky—from a UFO for all the evidence there is," he said, stifling a yawn and giving his scratchy eyes a rub. "There isn't a lot out there to go on to point me in any one direction, so I'm running around in circles. When I was out there this morning—"

"This morning?" Cruz exclaimed, cutting him off. "Geez, man, it isn't even noon yet. You've been out there and back already?"

"Couldn't sleep," Joe said, not wanting to think of the long hours he'd spent twisting and turning before striking out on the highway just before dawn. "Besides, I wanted to catch first light, but I could have slept in for all the good it did. I drove a five-mile circle from where I found her—I even walked a good mile of it on foot and came up with nothing." He leaned forward, pointing his finger to emphasize the point. "Zilch, zip, nada! Not a tire track, a skid mark or a footprint. There was no sign of wreckage, no nothing."

Frustrated, he sank back in the chair, stretching his legs out in front of him and tilting his cowboy hat back on his forehead with the tip of his thumb. "Granted, that was one hell of a rainstorm last night and it's not like I went out there expecting to find a big sign pointing me in the right direction, but damn, if there'd been an accident or she'd broken down or had a flat tire, there was no sign of it—and no car."

"Maybe she just had a fight with her boyfriend?" Cruz said, snapping his fingers as the idea came to him. "She got out of the car and he drove off, left her there and by the time he got back, she was gone!"

"Possibly," Joe nodded, arching a brow. "But it doesn't explain the head injury."

Cruz sank back. "Oh, yeah."

"And it's not likely she gave herself a club on the head."

"Not very."

"Besides, why hasn't the guy reported her missing then?"

"Good point," Cruz acquiesced good-naturedly. "What about a robbery then? She could have been accosted, robbed—that would explain her injury, maybe even the memory loss."

"I thought of that—or a carjacking," Joe said, yawning again. "At least, that would be my bet at this point. But we're trying not to overlook anything—grand theft auto, kidnapping, missing persons but as of about thirty minutes ago, there have been no stolen vehicles reported and no one has reported her missing. So until that happens, or we find a car or some other piece of evidence, we wait."

"Well one thing's for certain," Cruz pointed out. "She sure as hell didn't walk out there—at least not in the shoes she was wearing. They may have been water soaked, but they were practically new."

"So that means somebody had to have taken her out there and purposely left her," Joe concluded, folding his arms across his chest. The thought had his frown deepening.

"Left her for dead," Cruz added quietly.

The sober thought rendered them both quiet for a moment. Joe remembered the terror he had seen in her eyes. It took more than an accident to put that kind of fear in a person's eyes.

"I guess that means you're looking at an attempted murder," Cruz stated.

Joe glanced up. Having someone trying to kill you would have you looking pretty damn scared. "Sorta looks that way, doesn't it?"

"Signs seem to be there," Cruz continued. "And it would explain the head injury, the lack of any evidence, any clues."

"Somebody took her out there," Joe said in a quiet voice, closing his eyes and seeing her panicked face in the darkness. "Somebody who wanted her dead."

"Have you been thoroughly poked and prodded?"
Rain looked up at the sound of Carrie's voice and

smiled. The portly nurse had been nowhere in sight when she'd returned to her room earlier after an exhausting series of tests and an examination by the doctor.

"Thoroughly," she said, pushing away her empty lunch tray. She wasn't sure about the rest of her, but her appetite certainly appeared to be healthy.

"Good," Carrie said, pushing her solid frame through the open doorway and floating quietly across the worn linoleum floor. "We don't feel people are doing their jobs around here unless they make our patients feel like pincushions."

Rain held out her arm, looking down at the row of bandages left from the various blood samples that had been drawn. "Then I think it's safe to say you've got hardworking people on your staff."

"And your examination with Dr. Martinez? That went okay?"

Rain thought of the tall, good-looking doctor and his kind, compassionate nature. "Yeah, it went all right. He took a lot of time, explained a lot of the things to me about my head injury and the memory loss. And he talked about possible prognosis and told me not to try to force myself to remember, that if things were going to come back, they'd come back in their own time."

"That's true. You can't push these kinds of things."

"But he also admitted there was a possibility I'd never recover my memory, or only bits and pieces of it."

"There's always that possibility," Carrie admitted. "But then, every prognosis has a worst-case scenario."

Rain smiled. "You sound just like the doctor."

"Oh, Lord, don't tell me that!" Carrie said with a cackle. Reaching out, she patted Rain on the arm. "You feeling a little better about things now?"

Rain laughed. "I'm not sure if I feel better or if I'm just tired of thinking about it. But the doctor was very kind—you've all been."

"Well, Cruz—he's the best. We may not have a lot to brag about here in Mesa Ridge, but we can brag about him," Carrie said, reaching for the lunch tray. "Why don't you try to take another little nap now. I'll get this out of the way—" She stopped as she glanced down at the empty tray. "Well, will you look at this— another clean plate. You know, if you aren't careful, those people in the kitchen are going to start thinking you like the food around here. Then we'll all have to suffer for it."

Rain smiled, liking the feeling and liking the sturdily built nurse and her no-nonsense manner. "I don't know what's the matter with me. I can't seem to get enough."

"Well, darlin', there's nothing the matter. This is exactly what you need," Carrie said, pulling a thermometer out of the cabinet beside the bed and giving it a violent shake. "Some regular meals and a whole lot of rest." She popped the thermometer into Rain's mouth. "I understand you managed to get in a short nap before lunch, too."

Unable to speak with the thermometer in her mouth, Rain nodded. There had been just enough time after she'd returned to her room after her appointment with the doctor for a catnap before they brought her lunch. It hadn't been a very long nap, just long enough for her mind and body to rest and her subconscious to dream and conjure up images of a man—tall, dark and mysterious. He had been reaching out to her with strong, powerful arms and she'd felt warm and secure in his embrace.

She had awakened from her nap feeling strangely comforted and calmed by the dream. Did she know the man? Was he someone from the life she'd forgotten, someone who would be looking for her?

"Then I'd say that's just what the doctor ordered," Carrie was saying in response to her nod. "A little rest and relaxation and you'll be as good as new." She pulled the thermometer from Rain's mouth and squinted to read it. "How's your head feeling?"

Rain touched the tender spot on the top of her head and winced. "Oh, it's still there."

Carrie's smile faded as she peered through her bifocals to take a look. "It certainly is." Shifting her gaze to Rain, her eyes narrowed. "How's the headache?"

"Still there, too," she admitted, sinking back against the pillows. "But better."

"Feel up to a little company?"

Rain sat up straight. Had someone come for her? Was she going to find out who she was and where she belonged?

"C-company? You mean someone—"

"The sheriff, sweetheart," Carrie added quickly. "Sheriff Mountain."

"The sheriff," Rain said in a small voice. Feeling the sting of tears, she quickly looked away. "I thought..."

"I'm sorry, dear, I—" Carrie reached out, giving her hand a squeeze. "I wasn't thinking."

"It's okay," Rain assured her even though a large tear spilled onto her cheek.

Carrie squeezed her hand again. "Why don't I tell him to come back a little later? Maybe this isn't the best time…."

"No, that's okay," she insisted, swiping at the tear. "Tell the sheriff to come in. I'd like to see him. I'd at least like to thank him."

Carrie regarded her for a moment. "You sure you're up to this?"

Rain nodded, giving her a small smile. "Absolutely."

Carrie looked unconvinced. "Okay, if you're sure."

"Carrie," Rain said, stopping her as she started toward the door. "Sheriff Mountain—he's the one who gave me my name, isn't he?"

Carrie nodded. "Yes, he did. You going to give him a hard time about that?"

Rain smiled and shook her head. "No, I like my name."

Carrie smiled, too, and turned back toward the door. "You talk to the sheriff and I'll see what I can do about finding you a little something sweet to tide you over until dinner. Okay?"

Rain felt herself smiling again. "You'll get no argument from me."

She watched as Carrie sailed out the door and down the corridor, then sank back against the pillows and closed her eyes. She thought of the dream she'd had, thought of the man who had held her and made her feel wanted and safe. Had the tall stranger come looking for her? Would he hold her and whisper to her and make everything feel better again? Would he give her back her name, her identity, her life?

"Hello."

Chapter 3

Rain opened her eyes and felt every nerve in her body come to full alert. She didn't know what she'd expected when Carrie had told her the sheriff was there to see her, wasn't even sure she had any sort of expectation at all. Somewhere in the back of her brain she'd conjured up images of a badges and uniforms and guns in black holsters, but whatever she'd imagined, a tall Native American with long black hair and dark, haunting eyes wasn't it.

She realized in that moment the stranger from her dreams, the man to whom she had turned to for comfort, the man who had held her and in whose arms she had felt so secure was a stranger no longer. He wasn't someone from her past, someone who could tell her who she was and where she belonged. The stranger from her dreams was from the here and the now. He wasn't someone she'd imagined or made up in her head, he was real—and he had a name and a face.

"Sheriff Mountain."

He stood in the doorway, his broad shoulders and powerful frame all but swallowing up the space.

"Joe Mountain," he said by way of introduction.

"And I'm...well, I'm Rain," she said with a small laugh. She sat up, pushing a hand through her hair and wondering what she'd done with the comb Carrie had given her. "But I guess you already know that since I understand you're the one who named me."

If he was embarrassed, or pleased by the acknowledgment, it didn't show in his expression. In fact, nothing showed on his hard, lean face and Rain felt herself growing tense.

"May I come in?" he asked politely.

Her first reaction had been to refuse, to put him off and turn him away, but that was not only unreasonable, it was irrational. For some thoroughly inexplicable reason, she found herself hesitant, reluctant—almost shy about facing him.

She couldn't explain it. The whole thing was crazy. The man was only there to help her, was probably her best hope at putting her life back together. She had nothing to fear from him. He'd found her in the desert, had gotten her the help she'd needed. At the very least, she needed to thank him for saving her life. And besides that, she needed to talk to him, she *wanted* to talk to him. She had questions she'd hoped he could answer, concerns she'd hoped he'd address. So what was her problem? Why was her throat freezing up and the palms of her hands turning moist?

The dream. That stupid, silly little dream she'd had during her nap. He'd been in it, had been the tall dark stranger in her dream, the one who had touched her and held her and made her feel safe and warm. She felt like she knew him, like she meant something special to him and that was ridiculous. She felt embarrassed. The man was a stranger to her and she to him and there was nothing special about that.

"Of course," she said, doing as best she could to push her apprehension aside. "Please do come in."

Even though his khaki uniform was contemporary and looked appropriately official, Sheriff Joe Mountain had a rugged, distinctive look. Holding a weathered black cowboy hat in his hands, his dark hair pulled into a ponytail down his back, he looked like he belonged to a wilder, more uncivilized time.

Nothing about him was reserved or unsure. He crossed the room with strong, bold steps—each one speaking of confidence and ability. A man on a mission, he knew what he wanted and went after it. This was his realm, his arena and you played by his rules. Mesa Ridge, Nevada, may be a million miles from nowhere, but it was definitely Joe Mountain's town.

"How are you feeling?" he asked as he crossed the room toward her.

"F-fine," she stammered, feeling heat rise in her cheeks and banking down her nerves. "I'm feeling fine, thank you."

"I understand you had quite a morning." It was a statement, not a question or an inquiry and there was nothing empathetic or particularly charitable in his tone. His voice was as devoid of emotion as his expression appeared to be.

"They ran tests, yes," she told him, brushing off the tedious hours in the lab with a casual wave of her hand. "And I saw the doctor again."

"I have a few questions, if you're feeling up to it— about last night. About what you remember."

"I'll do my best," she said with a small shrug, telling herself it was foolish to feel disappointed. This was the shadowy figure from her dreams, the one she'd hoped would come find her, the one she'd hoped would make her feel safe and secure again. Only he had found her and she was feeling anything but safe and secure now. "I just don't know how much help I'll be."

"I talked with Cruz—Dr. Martinez," he said, setting his hat on the nightstand beside the bed and reaching for a tablet from the pocket of his shirt. "He's given me a pretty clear picture of your injuries and the memory loss."

"Yes," she mumbled, picturing the two men discussing her. The thought made her awkward, self-conscious. What had they said about her? What was it Joe Mountain had asked about her?

Turning away, she suddenly became distracted by the comb in the bed table. A lot of good it would do her now. She didn't know if she'd always been concerned about her appearance, but she seemed to be concerned about it now—or at least she was since Sheriff Mountain walked in.

"So just to clarify things, is it correct to say you have no memory of anything before waking up in the desert?"

She looked up at him, forgetting about the comb and her vanity. "That's right."

"Nothing?"

She thought of the black hole in her memory and slowly shook her head. "Not a thing."

"So you don't have any idea why you might have been out in such a remote area, don't know how you got there?"

"That's right."

He flipped through the pages of his tablet. "Let's talk about the desert, then. Why don't you tell me the first thing you do remember?"

She closed her eyes, trying not to think about the gnawing fear she remembered. "The rain."

He looked up from his notes. "The rain?"

She nodded. "Against my face. I was lying there looking up at the clouds and it kept getting in my eyes."

"So you were on the ground?"

Rain opened her eyes and looked up at him. "I guess I was. I never thought about it really, but I guess you're right. I was lying on the ground."

"As though you'd fallen?"

She thought about it a moment, then shook her head. "I don't think so. At least, I don't remember falling." She gave her head another shake and shrugged. "But then I suppose I could have. I don't really remember."

"And after that? You were lying looking up at the clouds and it was raining. What happened then?"

She closed her eyes again. "I remember my head hurting and when I got to my feet I felt dizzy."

"Did you see anything then—around you I mean? Was there anyone with you? Was there a car there? Any people?"

She opened her eyes, knowing she would never forget the cold, desolate feeling she'd had. "No, nothing."

He thought for a moment, then made a notation in the tablet. "You were near the highway?"

"No," she said, looking up at him. "I—uh—I remember because I didn't know which way to go. It was raining so hard and the ground was wet and muddy." She didn't like thinking about how lost and alone she had felt or how faint and ineffectual her screams had sounded. "I just started to run."

Something flashed in his eyes when he looked at her, something she would have sworn was soft and compassionate, but it was so fast and so fleeting, she couldn't be sure.

"So you pretty much just stumbled upon the highway?"

"Pretty much. I had no idea where I was. It was getting darker and I confess, the thought of being out there alone in the middle of the night..." A clutch of emotion had the words catching in her throat and she put her head back against the pillows.

"Are you all right? Need something?"

She shook her head, taking several deep breaths and feeling her composure restoring. "No, I'm fine, honestly. I just don't like...it's a little difficult to think about it. Coming to like that, in the middle of nowhere and not remembering..."

Once again emotion had her strangling on the words and she squeezed her eyes tight against the sting of tears. "I'm sorry, Sheriff, I'm not normally so emotional...." She realized what she'd said and looked up at him, feeling almost as lost and as helpless as she had out in the desert. "At least I don't think so," she said with a humorless laugh. "But the truth is, I don't know. I don't remember."

Joe reached for a box of tissues from the nightstand and offered them to her. "We could do this another time, if you like. Maybe when you're feeling a little stronger."

"No, I'm fine," she insisted, pulling tissues from the box. Everything about him spoke of strength and courage, of power and determination. She felt weak crying in front of him and for reasons she didn't quite understand, she didn't want him to think of her as weak. "It just bothers me to think about it, to not be able to remember. It's very…frustrating."

It was also very terrifying, but she didn't feel she needed to make that confession.

"That's understandable." He walked to the chair beside the bed, gesturing to it. "May I?"

"Oh, please, yes," she said, blotting her cheeks dry. "Sit down."

He pulled the chair close and lowered his tall frame into it. "So once you'd come to, you'd started walking."

"That's right." Her nose was stuffy and probably needed a good blowing, but that phantom vanity had her refraining from doing so. It was bad enough that her hair was snarled and her face was completely devoid of makeup.

"Do you have any idea how long you might have walked around out there?"

Rain remembered the bitter cold and her aching muscles. "It seemed like forever. I can't really say, but it seemed like a long time."

"Hours do you think?"

"At least."

"And you were walking that whole time."

"Except when I ran."

He looked up from his tablet. "Ran?"

"Like in circles," she confessed. "Panic, I guess."

"I suppose that would be understandable, too."

She watched as he looked down at the tablet again and started writing. She suspected the acknowledgment was about as close to sympathy she was going to get from him.

"Before you reached the highway, do you remember anything about the surrounding landscape? Were you heading toward the mountains? Did you see any large rocks? Anything like that?"

She thought for a moment. "Not really. It was dark and nasty because of the storm, of course." She closed her eyes and thought for a moment longer. "Oh, wait," she said, her eyes popping open. "I do remember seeing mountains in the distance."

"Okay," he said, jotting in his notebook. "And when you were walking, were you walking toward the mountains, or away from them?"

"I walked toward them."

He made another notation in the tablet, his head bent in concentration. "So when you reached the highway, which way did you turn? Right or left?"

Rain thought for a moment. "I think it was right."

He looked up. "You think?"

"It was right—I'm pretty sure." She hesitated, watching as he continued to write. "Why? Is it important, Sheriff?"

He lowered his tablet. "I don't know. Just trying to get a better idea about where you were out there. I know where you were when I found you. Trying to see if I could retrace your steps."

"I see."

"So you turned right?" he asked again. "You're pretty sure."

She closed her eyes, trying to relive the moment again. "It was right," she said, opening her eyes. "I remember now because I thought I'd seen a light coming from that direction."

"A light? You mean like a headlight? A porch light? Streetlight?"

"No," she said, shaking her head. "It was more like a flash—like the sun hitting something shiny."

"Except it was raining."

She shrugged meekly. "You're right. I'm sorry."

"Don't apologize. You've given me something to go on here."

"I have?" she asked, feeling ridiculously pleased.

"Sure."

He did something then that had her heart actually leaping in her chest. He smiled. Not a full-out smile, but a small, funny little one that nearly knocked her socks off.

"Oh," she said with a nervous laugh. "Good."

He nodded, no trace of the smile showing now, and made another notation in the tablet. "Okay, good." Looking up, he leaned back in the chair. "What does Logan mean?"

She sat up. "Logan? I don't know. Why?"

"It doesn't sound familiar, doesn't ring any bells?"

Her eyes grew wide. "Is that my name?"

He glanced up from the tablet again. "I don't know. You kept saying it over and over in the car last night."

"Logan," she repeated slowly, trying to tell if the name sounded familiar on her tongue. "Logan."

"Well?"

She sank back against the pillows. Her head began throbbing again and she remembered what Dr. Martinez had said about forcing the memories.

"No," she said with a tired sigh. "I don't know what it means. It doesn't sound familiar to me." A sudden thought had her sitting up again. "But it could mean something, couldn't it? I mean, maybe it's a...a clue."

"It's something to look into," he admitted, but it

was obvious he wasn't sharing her enthusiasm. With the flip of his wrist, he swung the tablet closed and rose to his feet. "I think that's it for the time being. I'll let you get back to your rest." Reaching into the breast pocket of his shirt, he pulled out a card. "If you think of anything else—anything, it doesn't matter how small or unimportant it may seem—my number is right there. Give me call, day or night."

Rain stared down at the card. Seeing his name printed neatly in bold black letters, she felt something tighten in her chest. "I will, thank you."

"Did you have any questions for me?"

She thought for a moment, glancing up from the card. "Why Rain?"

For the first time he looked something less than controlled, as though the question had caught him off guard.

"It's Navajo," he mumbled, reaching for his hat. "An old legend. Rain Woman, born of the elements." Holding his hat by the brim, he looked down at her. "You don't like it?"

"I do like it," she said, her voice feeling strangely tight in her throat. "I like it very much."

"Good," he murmured. There it was again, that small, funny little smile—there only for a moment, before disappearing again. "Anything else?"

She nodded. "What do you think happened out there in the desert? Why do you think I was out there?"

He looked at her for a moment, his black eyes devoid of any emotion, of any expression at all. It was as if she had asked him about the weather.

"At this point, I couldn't even offer a guess," he said in a low voice.

She was too disappointed to be angry, too frightened

to argue. "I have to find out who I am, Sheriff," she said, looking up at him and not bothering to hide the tears she felt stinging her eyes now. "I *have* to."

"I know," he said, taking a step closer to the bed. "And you can be damn sure I'm not going to rest until we do."

His words were softly spoken, but full of intensity and she didn't doubt for a moment that he meant every word. She knew in that moment that Sheriff Joe Mountain was going to solve the riddle of her past, was going to conquer the darkness and would bring her to the light again.

With a stiff little bow, he turned and headed for the door.

"Sheriff," she called after him, bringing him to an abrupt halt. "Just one more thing."

He turned around. "Yes?"

"Thank you."

"You're sure?"

"It's right there in black and white," Deputy Ryan Samsung said, pointing to the faxed report he set on the desk. "No matches. There's been no one with the name of Logan matching the description of your Jane Doe reported missing."

Joe stared down at the papers on the desk. The report had merely been a formality, confirming what his gut had been telling him from the beginning. This wasn't a simple missing person's case and it was going to take more than punching a few things into a computer to figure this out.

He had a sense for these things and his sense was that something more was going on here, something menacing and dark and nothing about it was going to be simple. Whatever had happened in the desert had been dramatic and devastating and it had not only changed Rain's life, but his life, too.

"And you cross-referenced it with the State Department of Justice as well as the FBI?"

"Came up with nothing," Ryan assured him. "Just like you said."

"Well, it might have been nice to have been surprised for a change," Joe admitted, picking up the faxed report and slipping it inside a large manila folder. "But at least now we can be sure." He leaned back in his chair, glancing up at Ryan. "Did Gracie e-mail a description out to the newspapers in Sparks and in Reno?"

Ryan shook his head. "Gracie's not here."

Joe sat up. "What do you mean she's not here? Where is she?"

Ryan shrugged as he started for the door. "I don't know. I think she said something about a doctor's appointment."

That triggered a vague recollection in his brain and Joe breathed out a silent curse. Nothing had been the same around there since the young woman he'd hired to help out around the office had discovered she was pregnant. Files had piled up, faxes had gone unsent and the phones were ringing off the hook.

"Again? Didn't she just have one?"

"Don't ask me," Ryan said, raising his hands in surrender. "The woman's going to have a baby, who knows what goes on with that?"

"Then maybe you could e-mail that out."

"Oh, no," he said, reaching for his hat from a hook on the hat stand. "I don't know anything about that Internet stuff."

"It's not Internet, it's e-mail," he explained. "It's like typing a letter."

"Don't make no difference to me," Ryan insisted, shaking his head. "I don't mess with any of the cyber stuff." He slipped his hat on over his shaggy black hair and turned back to Joe. "Besides, I'm heading across town. Those drivers from the old mine have been barreling down Wheeler Road again and when school lets out that place is just an accident lookin' for a place to happen."

"What if I pull rank on you?"

"You won't," Ryan said, his eyes all but disappearing as his smile grew wider. "Because you know I don't know how to type."

"You've got two fingers, don't you?" Joe called after him as Ryan disappeared out the door and into the small parking lot outside.

He was annoyed, but not at Ryan. Not even at Gracie. He was angry at himself, angry that he was losing perspective and he couldn't seem to do anything to stop it.

In all their official documents and queries, she was listed as Jane Doe, but she was Rain to everyone else. She was the woman who had stepped out of the wilds of a storm and took refuge in his arms, the woman he couldn't stop thinking about, the woman he couldn't get out of his mind.

He'd been the law in Mesa County for over a decade and he'd seen his share of crime and unrest during that time. He'd investigated cases that upset him, that made him mad. He'd even had cases he'd taken personally, but none of those compared to this. Rain was different. He'd known it the moment she'd looked at him.

She may not remember what had happened to her

out there in the desert, but the memory of it had been there in her eyes. They'd had a harrowing, haunted look so clear and so frightening, it had sent a chill rattling through him.

He thought of that moment when she'd walked out of the gloom, when for a moment the clarity of the horror flashed like a beacon on her face. Something had passed between them then, something significant and profound. He'd not only seen the terror in her eyes, he had felt it and it had left him shaken.

He flipped the manila file closed and pushed himself away from the desk. He had to take a break, had to get away from this for a while. He was less than twenty-four hours into this investigation and already he could feel himself becoming lost, feel himself losing focus, losing touch.

Slowly he rose to his feet, heading out of his office toward the small break room just down the hall.

"Damn," he cursed in a low voice as he rounded the corner and spotted the empty coffee carafe. No filing, no e-mail and now no coffee. He only hoped once Gracie had her baby and got back to work things would finally get back to normal.

Grumbling, he walked to the sink and filled the coffee carafe with water, poured it into the drip coffeemaker and filled the filter with fresh grounds. But he grew restless waiting for the coffee to brew and wandered back out through the hall and to the outer office.

He stopped at Gracie's desk, looking at the computer. Reaching down, he tapped the mouse, bringing the screen to life, and called up the Internet messaging service. Maybe with a little caffeine running through his veins, he could give those e-mails a try. He was the sheriff and this was his office and like it or not, it was his responsibility to see to it that *everything* got done, no matter how small or how mundane—even if that meant he had to do it himself.

The truth of the matter was, this was his county, his piece of the planet and he had a stake in everything that went on in the sprawling two hundred miles of territory. When something went wrong or somebody got hurt, he took it personally.

And somebody had hurt Rain. They may not have stabbed her, or raped her or even beaten her up, but the pain on her face had been so great, it had managed to find its way to him, as well. He had felt it, just as sure and if he'd been the one abandoned. He had nothing to go on, no leads to pursue or clues to follow but somehow, someway he was going to find out who had injured her and why.

It may be his job to help her, but it was also the right thing to do, the only decent thing to do. The woman was alone in the world; she had no one to lean on, no one to calm and comfort her. She was the stuff legends were made of, the object of myth and lore. She was Rain Woman, born of the elements and christened by the rain. Like the tales from his ancestors, she had walked out of the desert, a mysterious woman with no past, no people and no one to protect her—and into his arms. It was not only his duty to help her, it was his destiny.

Reluctantly he sat down at the desk and slowly started composing the e-mail he wanted to send, but with his hunt-and-peck style on the keyboard, progress was slow and he soon grew restless. He wanted the information sent to the newspapers and media as soon as possible, but at this rate it was going to take forever.

He pushed away from the desk, stretching the stiffness in his arms and back. He needed something to help him, something to boost his sagging spirits and tense muscles. But just as he rose to go pour himself a fresh cup of coffee, the telephone rang.

"Sheriff Mountain," he barked into the phone.

"Sheriff? It's me, Gracie."

Joe could hear the alarm in her voice. "Gracie, what's the matter? You sound terrible."

"Oh, Sheriff Mountain," she sobbed through the wire. "Sheriff, I'm so scared. It's my baby. The baby's in trouble."

"Trouble? Gracie, what are you talking about?"

He pressed the phone close, straining to hear through the sobs and tears. He made out something about tests and lab results, none of which meant much to him, but the culmination of them all meant complete bed rest for her for the remainder of her pregnancy.

"Jerry's trying to find someone who can come in with me while he's at work during the day," she explained, stopping only long enough to blow her nose loudly. "I have to stay flat for at least the next twelve weeks. I can't come back to work. What about my job? What about all my work?"

He could hear how overwhelmed she was and looked around at the reams of papers yet to be filed and felt a little overwhelmed himself.

"Don't worry about your job," he assured her. "It'll be here whenever you get back—and we'll get along just fine. You just concentrate on taking care of yourself and that baby."

Chapter 4

It wasn't him, she could tell that now. He was short and stocky and this man was huge, built like a football player with his enormous shoulders and powerful arms. No, she could relax, it wasn't him. She could walk a little slower, breathe a little easier.

She had to stop this, had to try to keep her wits about her. She couldn't afford to become paranoid, imagining him around every corner and behind every bush. This wasn't the time to let her imagination get the best of her. There was too much riding on her, too much depending on her keeping a calm head and not panicking.

Only, if it wasn't him, why was he still behind her? Why did he have such a harsh look on his face and why was he getting so close? It wasn't him and he was the only one she had to be afraid of, the only one she had to fear.

So if this man wasn't him, why was she so afraid?

He was a stranger, and yet he had such cold, black eyes when he looked at her.

"Logan," *he said in a voice that turned her blood to ice.*

"No," she groaned.

It wasn't him—it wasn't Logan—but when the hand clamped down hard on her shoulder, she'd realized he'd been sent by him.

"No," she groaned again. "Tell Logan no. Tell him I won't go."

Her voice sounded as small and as weak as it had in the desert, lonely and lost like a cry in the night. Fear rose up from her throat, choking her words, stealing her breath. She couldn't breathe, couldn't move, couldn't get away....

"*Logan. Logan.*"

Fear. Panic. And then, the darkness.

"Rain?"

The voice cut through the darkness, reaching through the layers of dreams and fragments of nightmares like a hand extended.

"Rain. Wake up, Rain."

Suddenly she was warm; the warmth obliterated the cold and the darkness. She forgot about the panic, she forgot about the fear. She didn't need to be afraid any longer. Like strong arms holding her, she knew she was safe.

"Wake up, Rain."

She blinked, the light stinging her eyes, until she realized she was staring up into his eyes.

"Sheriff Mountain."

"I heard you from the corridor," he said, straightening up and slipping his hands from her shoulders. "Bad dream from the sounds of it."

It was only then that she realized he'd been touching her, one hand on either of her shoulders.

"Yes," she croaked, suddenly remembering the dark images and the cold eyes of a stranger. "Yes, a dream—a very bad dream."

"You okay now?"

"Fine," she said with a nod, pushing herself up against the pillows. Actually, she was out of breath and her heart hammered wildly in her chest and her hospital gown was drenched with sweat. "I—I'm fine."

He reached for the pitcher of water beside the bed, pouring her a glass. "Here, drink this. You look like you could use it."

She took a sip, the water feeling cool and soothing along her scratchy throat. "Thanks." She pushed her hair back away from her face and took another drink. "Did you need to see me for something?"

"Not really," he said, picking up the pitcher and refilling her water glass. "I was here on some other business. I was just passing by the room when I heard you."

"I see," she murmured, taking another sip of water. It was foolish to be disappointed, foolish to think he'd come just to see her.

"You want to talk about it? The dream, I mean."

She thought of the awful face of the stranger in her dream and shook her head. "Not really."

"Would you mind?" he pressed, reaching into his pocket and pulling out his tablet. "Maybe there was something significant."

She glared down at his tablet, hating that it was always just business with him. "In a dream?"

"You never know," he said with a shrug. "Maybe

you can dream about what happened even if you can't remember it."

He was right, of course, and she couldn't let her vanity get in the way of solving the mystery of her past.

"There was someone, a man," she began. "A big man."

"Did he look familiar to you? Did you know him?"

"No, he was a stranger."

"You remember what he looked like? Could you describe him?"

She drew in a shaky breath. "Oh, yes."

"Unfortunately, we don't have a sketch artist in the county, but I could probably arrange to have one come down from Carson City. It would take a take day or two, though. Think if you jotted down a few notes to yourself you'd be able to remember enough to work with someone?"

That gruff, angry face was one she would have no problem describing. It was etched permanently into her memory—and one thing she actually wouldn't mind forgetting.

"I think so," she said, taking another sip of water. "Do you think my dreams could be important?"

"Hard to say," he hedged. "But, maybe subconsciously you're able to remember something." He made a few notations in his tablet. "Do you remember anything else? Anything about what happened in the dream?"

She remembered gasping for air, remembered struggling to get away. "I know I was afraid."

"Of the man?"

She stared at the glass of water, but she was seeing phantom, elusive images in her mind. "Not at first."

She looked up at him. "I was relieved—at least in the beginning. He wasn't who I thought he was, wasn't the man I was afraid of, the man I was running away from, but then…"

"Then?" he prompted her when her words drifted off.

"Oh." She jumped, her thoughts scrambling. "Then I realized he was after me, too. Chasing me, grabbing me." She gave her head a shake. "I guess I just dreamed everyone was after me."

"Have you had this dream before?"

She shook her head, thinking about the dream she'd had of him even before she'd met him. "Not this exact dream."

"But others like it?"

She nodded. "Several since last night."

"About being pursued?"

"Yes."

"Same man?"

"No."

"Think you could describe any of the others?"

"I don't know," she said, thinking of dark images and shadowy features. "I don't think so."

She felt stupid and frustrated. Nothing made sense. What seemed so frightening in her dreams seemed almost silly now that she thought about it.

"This man you were afraid of, the man chasing you. Was he Logan?"

She felt a chill run the length of her spine, leaving her feeling unsettled and disturbed.

"No."

"You called out the name Logan."

She looked up at him. "I did? Again?"

Joe nodded. "But this man wasn't Logan?"

Something registered in her brain, something from the dream. "No, he wasn't."

"How can you be so sure?"

"Because he was sent by Logan." She groaned, pounding a fist into the mattress. "This is crazy. It doesn't make sense." She closed her eyes, feeling a dull throb start to radiate from the tender area at the top of her head. "Logan. What's Logan? Who's Logan? I don't even know why I keep saying it. I wish I could remember." She opened her eyes, sitting up again. "It must mean something if I keep saying it."

"Maybe," Joe said.

"Or maybe it's just the name of a character in a book you once read, or a neighbor, or your third-grade teacher."

They both stopped and turned toward the door. Cruz reached into the pocket of his white jacket and pulled out a stethoscope as he walked into the room.

"I thought we had agreed you would wait for me at the nurses' station, Sheriff Mountain," he said, glowering at Joe.

"And I had every intention of doing that very thing," Joe insisted, bringing his hands up in surrender. "But your patient was having a nightmare. I heard her calling out from the corridor." He turned and glanced back at her. "I thought maybe she could use some help."

"A nightmare," Cruz said, the annoyance in his voice disappearing in his concern for his patient. Reaching for Rain's wrist, he felt for her pulse. "Another bad one?"

"About the same as the other," she confessed.

He looked down at her, running the backs of his

fingers across her forehead. "You feel clammy and
your heart's still racing."

"I dreamed the bogey man was out to get me," she
sighed with a humorless laugh. She was tired of thinking about the dreams, tired of thinking about what was
real and what wasn't, tired of trying to figure out what
was important and what was just idle fantasy—and
most of all she was tired of not knowing the difference.

"The bogey man, huh?" Cruz repeated dryly. "That
doesn't sound good." He turned an accusing glance at
Joe. "I hope you weren't badgering her with more
questions."

"She said she dreamed someone was after her," Joe
admitted. "I thought maybe she might have remembered something."

"Do you think that's possible, doctor?" she asked
hopefully, sitting up again. "Could I remember something in my dreams?"

"What I *think*," Cruz said calmly, putting a hand
on her shoulder and guiding her back against the pillows, "is that you had a dream."

"I know, but—"

"A dream," Cruz said, cutting her off and shooting
Joe a dark look before turning back to her again. "And
I told you I wanted you to get some rest, not be trying
to interpret every little thing that pops out of your subconscious."

"But it could have been something from my past,
couldn't it?" she insisted.

"It is highly unlikely."

"But it's a possibility," Joe pointed out.

Cruz shot him another dark look. "An unlikely
one." He turned to Rain again. "It was just a dream."
He leaned closer, his voice growing softer. "I know

this is scary, and I know you're anxious to remember but your memory is going to come back when it comes back—no sooner than that." He straightened back up. "But I do have some good news, though."

Good news. Yes, she could use some of that. "My tests?"

"Everything looks great—X rays, lab work—and that bump on your head is healing nicely. I'd like to keep you here for just a couple days longer, just for observation, but I don't see any reason why we couldn't release you after that."

Rain wondered if blood really could turn to ice because she was fairly certain hers just did. "You mean out of the hospital?"

"Day after tomorrow," Cruz said, his smile widening. "There's a friend I'd like you to see, a specialist up at the University Medical Center in Sparks. He's done a lot of work with patients experiencing amnesia, memory loss, but that can be done on an outpatient basis."

"You're releasing me," she murmured, the ice in her veins sending a shiver down her spine. A world that had begun for her only a little more than a day ago had shifted again. Except for the desert, the hospital was all she knew.

"Are you sure she's ready?" Joe asked.

"She's more than ready," Cruz assured him. "Of course, she's going to need to take it easy, get plenty of rest and—" he glanced back down at Rain "—I'm going to want to see you back here for regular checkups. Carrie will get you set up with a schedule of appointments."

She sat up, clutching at Cruz's arm as he wrote in

the chart. "But, Dr. Martinez, if you release me, where will I go? I've nowhere to go."

"We've got a few days," he assured her. "We'll work something out."

"But how?" she insisted, another kind of panic taking hold. "I don't know anyone here. I don't have any money, I don't have a job. I don't even know if I know how to do anything."

"Don't worry about it now," Cruz said. "County Services can work this out. They'll find a place—"

"No need to get them involved," Joe said, interrupting him.

"What do you mean?"

"County Services don't need to find her a place," he explained, flipping his tablet closed and slipping it into the pocket of his shirt. "She can stay with me."

"What?" Rain was sure she must not have heard him right. She'd thought he had said she could stay with him.

"I've got lots of room," he said, taking a step closer to the bed. "I've got a place for you to stay."

Joe reached for an icy bottle of beer from the six-pack beside him on the porch. Leaning back against the rail post, he twisted off the cap and stared out across the desert to the soft glow of lights below in the distance.

Mesa Ridge was asleep at this hour, but occasionally he would catch the flash of headlights as someone made their way down Main Street, heading out toward the highway.

To the left of town, the lights from Flo's Tavern flashed on and off with customary regularity, and he had to smile. It was Friday night and the place would be hoppin' for at least another couple of hours. Ryan would be out on patrol and by morning, the holding cells of the Mesa County Jail would be full with repentant citizens in on charges ranging from public drunkenness to driving under the influence to disturbing the peace. In various stages of hangovers, they would dutifully pay their fines in the morning, put in another hard week at work and be back at Flo's the next Friday night where the whole thing would start all over again.

Joe tossed the cap on to the step and put the bottle to his lips, taking a long, slow drink. But he didn't begrudge the group at Flo's their good time, even if it occasionally did end in a fistfight or barroom brawl— as long as nobody got hurt and everyone made up in the morning. Everybody deserved to blow off a little steam from time to time. Maybe that's what he needed to do—blow off a little steam. Maybe it would help him clear his head and stop him from doing rash, reckless things he knew he'd only come to regret later on.

I've got a place for you to stay.

His grandiose offer replayed itself over and over again in his brain. What had come over him? Had he lost his mind? He'd been telling himself all day that he was losing objectivity when it came to Rain, been cautioning himself to keep perspective and not get too involved. Unfortunately, his little lectures to himself hadn't helped much. Bringing the woman home, offering her a room in his house wasn't exactly backing off, wasn't exactly taking a step back.

He took another drink, finishing the bottle and tossing it onto the porch beside him. He leaned his head back against the post, following the headlights of a car in the distance as it made their way down Main Street and on to the highway, and felt the warmth from the alcohol seep through his system.

He hadn't gone to the hospital to see her, at least that's what he told himself. He'd told himself he'd gone there to talk to Cruz, to try to clarify some details and clear up a few questions he had about her injuries. But the truth of the matter was, a telephone call could have taken care of any questions he'd had. The truth of the matter was, he'd gone there hoping to see her.

He'd sat at Gracie's computer, laboriously typing in Rain's description in the e-mails and wanting to see her again, wanting to see if her eyes were as blue as he'd remembered, if her skin really did look as soft and as silky as he'd remembered.

He'd stood in the corridor outside her room trying to think of an excuse to go inside. It was only luck that he'd heard her calling out—if you could call a nightmare luck. But then, once he'd heard her cry, he hadn't been thinking about excuses. He'd been in the room and by her side before he'd had a chance to think at all.

He watched as the headlights slowly made their way down the highway. It was a lonely sight, two small specks of light in the blackness of the desert.

He'd grown up in the desert. It was part of him, part of his people and their past. It was their home, their church and where their legends began. He'd joined the navy wanting to get away from the desert, wanting to be on the water and away from arid landscape and grueling heat. Only, during his five-year stint aboard the aircraft carrier *Dakota,* all he could think about was getting back, back to the land that was a part of him.

His thoughts drifted back to Rain and he felt something tighten in his chest. Still, the desert could be a scary place, especially when you're lost and alone. He tried to think about how it must have been for her, waking up not knowing where she was or who she was. She'd lost more than her way in the desert, she'd lost herself as well. She'd been left with nothing to rely on, no one to turn to, nowhere to go.

And yet she'd fought back. It would have been easy to have just given up, to have simply given in to the elements and let them get the best of her, but she hadn't done that. It had taken courage to do what she had done, to strike out her own way, letting instinct and a will to survive guide her.

He reached for another bottle. The woman had guts, he had to give her that. He'd seen that courage today in the hospital. It was obvious she had been terrified by that nightmare, but she hadn't collapsed against him frantic and hysterical. Instead she had sucked it in; she'd bested the fear until she'd regained control and composure. In his line of work, he'd seen people fall apart at a lot less than what she'd been through, so maybe it wasn't so unusual that he found himself admiring her.

But admiration was one thing; offering the woman a room in his house was something else entirely.

Twisting the cap free, he tossed it onto the step beside the first one and took a drink. There had been women in his life since his divorce, but he didn't bring them to his house and he had no idea what had possessed him to do it now. Granted, with five big bedrooms, a living room, a den, a dining room, a breakfast nook and a loft, it wasn't like he couldn't afford the space. But this was his home, his castle, the place he came to get away from work, not bring it home with him.

His rustic ranch house and the five thousand acres of high desert land surrounding it had been a dream for as far back as he could remember. He'd saved every dime he could during his tour of duty to scrape enough together for a down payment. When he'd met Karen, he told her about his dream and had believed her when she'd said she'd wanted to make it her dream, too, that she wanted to help him raise purebred mustangs and share his life on the ranch.

The beer felt cool going down and he took another long drink. Leaning back, he watched the headlights as they turned off the highway and onto a side road. What a fool he'd been, thinking someone like Karen would be content with life on a ranch in Nevada. But he'd been so taken with her, he hadn't wanted to examine her motives too closely. Otherwise he would have seen that they'd had nothing in common, would have realized their relationship was doomed from the beginning.

Karen had been the only child of a navy admiral who had pampered and indulged his "little princess" her entire life. Her childhood had been so different from his own. Except for the navy, all he'd ever known was the poverty and privation of reservation life. Yet he'd been foolish enough to think love could bridge any gap—and who knows, maybe love could. The only problem was, Karen hadn't loved him.

It wasn't until after the wedding, after his discharge from the navy, and after the move back to Mesa Ridge that he discovered Karen was carrying a child—another man's child. Of course, he only had himself to blame. He'd been so swept away, so amazed that the admiral's daughter had wanted him, he hadn't stopped to question her motives or wonder why. He hadn't wanted to look beyond the immediate, hadn't wanted to question why she wanted him—but after their marriage it soon became painfully obvious. What Karen had wanted was a father for her child and a convenient marriage to help her save face with her family and friends.

He sat up, his interest inching up a degree as he watched the headlights in the darkness turn off the road and onto the drive toward his place. But even as he watched the lights draw closer, his thoughts drifted back to Karen, to the marriage he'd tried so hard to save. Even after he'd learned about the baby, he'd tried to make it work, tried to put his feelings aside for the sake of the baby she carried. But when the infant died in childbirth, things grew worse. Karen fell into a deep depression, hating everything about Mesa Ridge, and everything about him.

Taking another drink from the bottle, he swallowed hard. He could still hear her angry insults, still hear her shouting at the top of her lungs, calling him a "dirty Indian." But all that was history now. Karen was gone, the marriage was over and they both had gone on with their lives. If he bore a few scars in his reluctance to trust or to try again, then so be it. His life was comfortable, his job stimulating and his ranch all the excitement he would ever need.

The car turned up the gravel drive, slowing to a stop in front of the house. He knew the car, and the driver, and raised a hand in greeting as Cruz stepped out and started up the drive toward the porch.

"Got a little more of that firewater there, Chief?"

Joe picked up a bottle from the six-pack and tossed it to Cruz. "Making a house call, Doc?"

Cruz sat down on the top step opposite him, twisting the cap off the bottle. "I don't know, you tell me."

"I'm feeling fine." He raised his beer in a toast. "And after a few more of these, I'm going to be even better."

Cruz smiled, tossing the cap onto the step with the others. "We'll see how good you feel in the morning."

Joe finished his beer and stopped as he reached for another. "You've got a point there."

"And if I'm not mistaken, I believe you made a promise to be at the hospital bright and early in the morning."

Joe groaned. He hadn't forgotten, but the reminder was almost enough to have him reaching for another beer—almost. Tomorrow was going to be difficult enough to get through without having to deal with a hangover, too. For some reason, the mysterious Rain had a way of making him do things he normally wouldn't even think of doing and he was going to need a clear head to make sure it didn't happen again.

"Not to worry, Doc, I'll be there—bright and early."

"Oh, I'm not worried," Cruz said, taking a drink of his beer. Swallowing, he turned, nodding toward the inside of the house. "All ready for a houseguest?"

Joe thought about the new linens he'd bought on his way home and the food he'd stocked in the refrigerator. "Pretty much."

"That was very generous of you," Cruz said, turning back to him. "Offering to take her in and all."

Joe shrugged. He and Cruz had been friends for a long time and Cruz knew better than anyone just how unusual it was for him to invite a woman home.

"She had nowhere to go and there's no telling where

she would have ended up if County Services had gotten involved.'' He rolled the empty beer bottle back and forth between the palms of his hands. "God knows I've got plenty of room.''

Cruz nodded, taking another drink. "I know, I was concerned about calling in the county, too. I'd even thought of talking to Marcy about maybe having her come stay at our place for a few days.''

Joe let his head fall back against the rail post. If he'd only kept his mouth shut, if he hadn't leapt in without so much as a second thought, he wouldn't be in the situation he was now.

Mesa Ridge might be a small town, but it had a heart of gold. Word about her would have spread. Even if she'd had to spend a night or two in a county holding facility, somebody would have eventually come forward to help—someone other than him. Instead, he'd jumped the gun. He'd taken one look at that lost, vulnerable face of hers and like the cavalry riding over the hill, he'd come running to the rescue.

"Well, maybe she'd prefer that,'' Joe suggested, getting his hopes up. Maybe it wasn't too late to wiggle out of this after all. "I wouldn't mind.''

Cruz shook his head. "I don't think so. With Marcy trying that change of venue case up in Carson City and gone all the time, it might be a little uncomfortable. Marcy and I adore our little daughter but you know what a chatterbox Annie can be. She would have driven the poor woman to distraction.'' Cruz took another swig of beer, wincing as it went down. "I think she'd probably like it a whole lot better here. It's quieter and more private. The poor thing needs her rest.''

Joe sighed, and leaned his head back against the post. It had been worth a try.

"Like I said," he said with a deep sigh. "I've got plenty of room."

Cruz turned and looked at him, pausing for a moment. "I have to admit I was a little surprised when you offered. It does seem a little unusual for you."

"You sayin' I'm not a nice guy?" Joe joked. He knew exactly what Cruz was alluding to.

"You're nice enough I suppose," Cruz conceded. "Just not normally so involved." He finished his beer. "It's a little unusual for you, don't you think?"

Joe took a deep breath. *Unusual* was putting it mildly.

"Maybe," he shrugged, turning to look at the lights of Mesa Ridge once again. "But then it's a little unusual to have someone wander out of the desert who doesn't remember her name or how she got there."

"You're right about that," Cruz conceded, taking another drink of beer.

"And with someone so helpless, it's hard not to want to help."

Cruz leaned his head back and looked at the lights as well. "I don't know. I have a feeling most men would like to help that woman even under normal circumstances."

The flash of jealousy that twisted in Joe's stomach was as out of place as it was unexpected. "Aren't you forgetting you're a respectfully married man?"

"Decidedly and joyfully married," Cruz corrected with a smug smile. "Marcy and Annie are all the women I can handle." Tilting his head back, he gulped the rest of his beer. "Besides, I was talking about you."

Joe sat up. "Me? What about me?"

Cruz set the empty bottle down on the porch and

leaned forward. "Joe, come on, this is me—Cruz. Maybe everyone else will believe you're helping the woman out of sympathy or a sense of duty or whatever, but I know better." He hesitated again. "Don't you think I've seen the way you look at her?"

Joe pushed himself to his feet and climbed down the steps onto the drive. "Maybe you're seeing things that aren't there."

Cruz came slowly to his feet. "Am I?"

Joe slipped his hands into the back pockets of his jeans and turned around, looking up at Cruz. "No."

"You know, it isn't a crime to be attracted to someone," Cruz pointed out.

"Even if she's the subject of an official investigation?" He slipped his hands from his pocket, bending down and picking up a pebble from the dirt drive. "I don't know what it is...there's just something about her.... I feel..." He tossed the pebble, sending it flying and disappearing into the darkness. "I can't explain it. Something terrible happened to her out there in the desert, someone hurt her—hurt her so bad she had to block it out in order to survive." He bent down and picked up another small stone, sending it flying. "And I can't tell you how that makes me feel." He turned and looked back at Cruz again. "If you could have seen the look in her eyes, if you could have seen the terror..." He shook his head. "It haunts me. And the thought of someone ever hurting...it makes me so furious, so angry...." He bent down and scooped up a handful of pebbles, hurling them out one after the other. "I told you, it makes no sense. I don't know if I'd call it attraction exactly, but for some reason I feel protective of her." He turned and looked at Cruz. "I want to protect her and I don't even know who she is.''

''You don't know who she is—*yet*,'' Cruz corrected. He slowly stepped down off the porch. ''But you will. And in the meantime, she can stay here with you and you two can get to know each other a little better.''

Frustrated, suspicious, apprehensive, Joe turned on his heels, spreading his arms and running out into the darkness. Staring up at the moon, he let out a loud yelp toward the night sky.

''What am I doing?'' he asked, calling back to Cruz. ''This isn't me. I don't do things like this, I don't get involved. I don't bring women here—not *here*.''

''Sometimes we don't have choices in these matters,'' Cruz pointed out quietly. ''And Rain isn't just any woman.''

Joe stared out into the darkness. As though in answer to his primal call, a coyote howled back from the blackness—a lost, lonely sound.

Cruz was right; Rain wasn't just any woman. She had a way of looking at him and changing everything. He wasn't just a man when he was with her; he became more than a man and that was the difference. She made him want to be better, want to aim higher, want to be different. His life changed the moment he saw her and he knew it would never be the same again.

Rain wasn't just any woman. But he still had to find out whose woman she was.

Chapter 5

"I think there's been some kind of mistake," Rain said, glancing down at the sweatshirt and jeans folded neatly on the bed. "These aren't my clothes."

"Sweetheart, I'm afraid the clothes you were wearing when you were brought in are a little worse for wear," Carrie said, reaching for a hairbrush and a comb from the bed stand and slipping them into a brown paper bag. "Besides, Sheriff Mountain wanted them."

Rain looked up. "Sheriff Mountain?"

Carrie nodded, putting several small bottles of shampoo and lotion into the paper bag, too. "For evidence, I guess."

"Evidence," Rain murmured, glancing down at the clothing again. She had to remember she was merely a case to Joe Mountain—a *charitable* case at that—a missing person who needed to be reported upon and investigated. She couldn't let herself misconstrue his offer of a room and board. Anything could have happened out there in the desert. It would make sense that he'd want to keep her close, would want to keep an eye on her. After all, it could turn out that *she* was the criminal and he'd have to arrest her then.

She closed her eyes, trying to block out all the awful scenarios that had played through her head in the last forty-eight hours. The shock and the panic of the amnesia hadn't disappeared, but it had subsided enough to allow her to think about things, to wonder and imagine. She wondered who she was, what kind of person she was. In her mind, she'd pictured herself anything from a lost member of the royal family to one of the FBI's Most Wanted and she couldn't help wondering when she finally did regain all those lost memories, when she finally did remember who she was, would she still feel the same?

"Your head bothering you?"

She opened her eyes to find herself looking into Carrie's kind, weathered face.

"No, I'm fine," she lied. "Just a little tired."

"Would you like some help getting dressed?"

Rain liked Carrie, liked how her tough, no-nonsense tone could soften in a moment's notice, how her stern, rigid expression could transform to reveal a woman capable of tremendous compassion.

"No, I'm fine," she insisted, shifting a swell of emotion. "But thank you. And thank you for these." She reached for the clothes on the bed, catching them up in her arms. "It was very thoughtful of you."

"Well, we couldn't exactly send you out of here in your hospital gown," Carrie said, her smile broadening. "But you'd better thank Sheriff Mountain."

Rain's eyes opened wide. "Oh?"

Carrie nodded, setting the bag of toiletries down on to the bed. "He's the one that brought them in. Dropped them off at the nurses' station a little while ago." She took the sweatshirt from Rain's hands and unfolded it, holding it up to size it on her. "Not exactly the latest from Paris, but at least your backside won't be flapping around in the breeze." Holding the sweatshirt up, she turned it around, examining front and back. "If I'm not mistaken, I think these are some of Karen's things."

Rain felt a chill. "Karen?"

"Karen Mountain," Carrie said, folding the shirt and handing it to her again. "Joe's wife."

Rain wasn't sure if she had consciously intended to sit down on the bed or if her knees had simply buckled beneath her. *His wife.* The words echoed through her brain like a cry through a desert canyon.

He was married. Joe Mountain was married. She would be staying with the Sheriff and his...wife.

"I see," she murmured, but her voice sounded hollow and distant in her ears.

"Like I said, they'll do for now," Carrie continued, handing her back the sweatshirt. "We'll see about getting you some of your own things soon."

Rain wondered if she was suffering from another bout of amnesia since she had no real recollection of taking off her hospital gown and slipping into Mrs. Joe Mountain's clothes. She'd performed the motions needed to make the transformation in a trance, feeling shell-shocked and dazed.

It was stupid to feel disappointed. After all, it should hardly matter if he was married. It wasn't as though they were friends. She barely knew him—she barely knew anyone—and the only thing they'd ever talked about was her "case."

So why was she feeling hurt? Why was she feeling as though he'd kept the truth from her? Was it part of the amnesia that had her clinging to any small kindness she was shown? Was it part of the illness that had her misconstruing intentions and blowing everything out of proportion?

He was a sheriff, a lawman doing is duty—nothing more and nothing less. He'd been all business, all procedure, and she was a case to him, a mystery that needed to be solved. Still, he had gone an extra mile, stepped out on a limb when he'd offered her a place to stay and his gesture was kind and compassionate. He was doing his job, doing the right thing. She was the one who was having difficulty keeping things in perspective.

"Hey, those look pretty good on you. Go take a look," Carrie said, motioning to the mirror in the bathroom as she gathered the hospital gown off the bed. "And they look a whole lot better than this thing."

Rain walked into the small bathroom, staring at herself in the mirror above the sink. They weren't a perfect fit, but the clothes were an improvement on the faded hospital gown she'd been wearing. Still, she felt pathetic standing there in another woman's clothes.

She was no one—a woman with no name, no memories. The sheriff felt responsible for her, felt pity for her and he and his wife were taking her in, offering her room and board because she had no where else to go.

"What a fool you are," she mumbled to her reflection in the mirror.

"Who's a fool?" Carrie asked, walking up behind her.

Rain jumped, her gaze shifting to Carrie's reflection in the mirror.

"Uh, me," she stammered, turning away. Stepping past Carrie, she walked back to the bed, busying herself with straightening the sheets and pillows. "It's silly to worry about how I look. What difference does it make?"

Carrie laughed, peering at her own reflection and giving her gray curls a casual swipe with her hand. "Oh, darlin', a woman is always concerned with how she looks. My goodness, I've seen women come out of anesthesia after major surgery and ask for lipstick and a mirror." She turned back, walking out of the bathroom. "But we're women, and like it or not, it's in our nature to want to look our best."

"I suppose," Rain conceded with a smile.

"And just for your information," Carrie added. "You don't have to."

Rain stopped as she reached to fluff another pillow. "I don't have to what?"

Carrie laughed and leaned close. "Worry. You look great."

Embarrassed, Rain couldn't stop the smile this time. "I do?"

"And you don't have to do that, either," Carrie insisted, taking the pillow from Rain and tossing it down on the bed. "This is a hospital, not your mother's house. We have people who do the linens for us."

Rain glanced down at the bed, surprised to find the sheets smooth and straight and the pillows fluffed. "Oh! I didn't realize...I mean...I guess I wasn't thinking...."

Carrie chuckled, slipping a supportive arm around Rain's shoulders. "It's okay, sweetie. You're a little nervous—I don't blame you. It can be a cold, cruel world out there, but don't you worry. You're in Mesa Ridge now and nothing bad is going to happen to you here. The sheriff is going to take good care of you and you're going to like it out there on his ranch. It's peaceful and beautiful—and he's got himself some nice-looking horseflesh. Ever been horseback riding?"

"I—I don't know," Rain admitted honestly.

"Well, you'll learn," Carrie assured her, giving her shoulders a pat. "You'll learn. Just try not to worry. Everything's going to be fine."

"I, uh, I guess I am a little nervous," Rain confessed, suppressing the desire to straighten the bed linens again. She was getting out of the hospital, taking the first steps toward getting her life back and she should be feeling good about it. Instead she was feeling emotional and upset, like she was on the verge of tears. "I feel so helpless—and I don't want to be a bother to anyone. I don't want to impose on the Sheriff and his wi—"

"Well, look at you." Cruz's voice boomed loud at the door, drowning out everything else and surprising them both. Rain and Carrie turned as he sailed into the room with a chart tucked under his arm. "I'd say you look like you're ready for your walking papers."

"She's raring to go," Carrie announced, giving Rain a supportive pat on the back. "We're just waiting on the sheriff. Have you seen him? He was by the nurses' station earlier, but I don't know where he went after that."

"He's using the phone," Cruz said, reaching for Rain's wrist and taking her pulse. "There was some problem at the office. Gracie's not working anymore and—''

''All set?'' Joe asked, walking into the room.

His dark gaze zeroed in on her from across the room and Rain felt her entire body flush with heat. He was married, so why was looking at her like that, why was there such hunger in his eyes, such yearning? Surely she wasn't imagining that.

''Any special instructions?'' Joe asked, turning to Cruz.

''Just make sure that she gets lots of rest,'' Cruz instructed, slipping the chart from under his arm and flipping it open. ''And plenty to eat.'' He glanced up at Rain as he jotted in the chart. ''Which probably means you should avoid anything Joe fixes. I've eaten his cooking.''

Rain looked from Cruz to Joe and back again, feeling her cheeks flush even brighter. The teasing embarrassed her considering the sheriff would no doubt turn the mundane chore of her care over to his wife.

''I'll try to remember that,'' she said in a small voice.

''And you're going to make sure she gets up to Sparks for her appointment with Dr. McGhan,'' he said, turning to Joe.

''Thursday at ten-fifteen, right?''

''Right,'' Cruz agreed, flipping the chart closed.

''Isn't there a bus or something I could take?'' Rain asked, stepping hesitantly off the bed. She felt helpless and ineffectual standing there and letting others take control of her life. The man and his wife had offered her a place to stay; she didn't want to replace their kindness by becoming a burden. ''I'm putting the sheriff out enough as it is.''

"There's a bus, but believe me, you don't want to be on it," Carrie said with a laugh, giving her shoulders a squeeze. "It would be no place for you. It's the gamblers' special that comes through here from Salt Lake."

"I wouldn't mind," she insisted, turning to Carrie and then to Joe. "Honestly."

"You're not taking the bus," Joe stated flatly.

"But I hate to inconvenience you any more than I—"

"It's not an inconvenience." He sounded almost irritable. "I wouldn't have offered if it was."

His sharp tone had her feeling even more foolish and embarrassed. Of course, she wasn't an inconvenience. She was just part of the job.

"Then maybe there's something else I could do," she insisted. "Maybe help around the house?"

Just then his beeper went off and he scowled, reaching down to check the small message it transmitted. "The only thing I need is someone to answer the phone."

Suddenly he froze, slowly raising his head and turning to Cruz. "What about restrictions, Doc? Is there anything the lady shouldn't be doing?"

"I guess that's up to the lady," Cruz said, turning to her. "Do what you feel up to, just don't try to overdo. And don't let Joe put you to work pitching hay or cleaning stalls."

"No stalls," Joe agreed. "But what about telephones?"

Cruz snapped his fingers now. "Gracie!"

Joe looked at Cruz and nodded. "What do you think?"

"I think it's a great idea."

"Wait!" she demanded, stepping between them. "Have I missed something here? What are you talking about?"

"At my office—the sheriff's office, our receptionist Gracie is out on maternity leave and I thought, if you're interested and you feel up it, you might want a part-time job?"

Rain wasn't sure if she felt relieved or upset. Living at the sheriff's house would be difficult enough, but working with him might prove to be more than she could handle. Still, the thought of working and keeping busy appealed to her. It would get her out of the house and make her feel a little useful.

"I don't know about a lot of things," she said after a moment. "But I think I still remember how to answer a phone."

"It's so dry."

Joe brought the car to a stop at the signal and turned to the woman in the passenger seat. "Did you say something?"

Rain pointed out the window. "I couldn't help notice, it's so hot and dry—not a cloud in the sky. Hard to believe just a few days ago it was raining."

The picture of her appearing out of those driving sheets of rain flashed in his brain. "The weather can be pretty volatile out here when it wants to be."

Her gaze followed several pedestrians as they crossed in the walk in front of the Jeep. "And Sheriff, I, uh, I wanted to thank you for the clothes. Carrie told me you brought them."

Joe turned, looking at the sweatshirt and jeans he had taken from the large trunk of clothes Karen had never bothered to take with her. "They're not much. I had to send your things up to the state crime lab for analysis."

"Evidence," she murmured, turning to look out the car window.

"Well, they're only evidence if it's determined a crime has been committed," he pointed out.

"I see," she said, turning to look out the window again. "Do you think there was?"

He turned, watching as she stared out the window. She'd barely looked at him this morning and their conversation since they'd gotten in the car had little more than idle chitchat.

He wasn't sure what he'd expected, didn't know how he'd thought she would act going home with him for the first time. He'd imagined she would be nervous because God knows he was. And he suspected she might have a few misgivings. But was it so completely out of the realm of possibility that she might also have been just a little bit excited? She was, after all, being released from the hospital. That was a good thing, wasn't it?

"Hard to say," he said after a moment. "We don't have a lot to go on at this point." The signal turned green and he turned and started slowly across the intersection. "We'll see what we come up with after you meet with the sketch artist tomorrow, but what I'd like, if you're up to it, is to drive out to the area where I found you. We could try to retrace your steps, maybe see if something looks familiar or if it triggers anything."

"Absolutely, I'd like that," she said, turning to him. "And if there is anything else you can think of that might be helpful—I don't know, look through mug shots, old newspaper reports…whatever—I'm willing to do that, too.'' She turned, glancing back out the window. ''I'll do anything to find out who I am.''

For just a moment, there had been a burst of life in her eyes, a look of hope and anticipation and it almost made him feel guilty. Cruz had been adamant about her not getting her hopes up, cautioning her again and again not to try to force herself to remember. He hoped he wasn't raising her hopes too high by taking her back into the desert.

''Well, like I said, it was just a thought.''

''Were you serious about needing help at the sheriff's office?'' she asked. ''Or is this just something to keep me busy?''

He found the fact that she doubted him mildly insulting. ''You don't believe me?''

''I believe you're very nice and your offer is more than generous. I just don't want to put you to any more trouble. I really can take care of myself. I don't want to get in the way.''

Why didn't she just slap him across the face? ''It's not a matter of getting in the way. And I'm not that nice.''

''Then you really do need help.''

As if on cue, his pager went off. ''Help. I need someone to rescue me.'' He shot her a glance. ''Look, you don't have to feel obligated. If you're not interested, it's no big deal. I just thought—''

''No, no, it's great,'' she insisted, cutting him off. ''I want to help.''

''Then it's settled,'' he murmured, feeling as though it were anything but.

''As long as you're sure.''

''I'm sure,'' he insisted. ''But you may not be once you see what you've gotten yourself into.''

She smiled, but her smile froze and quickly fell. "I just thought of something." She turned to him. "What if I don't know how to do anything?"

"Believe me, it doesn't take a memory to answer the phone," he assured her. "All you gotta know is how to say 'hello.'"

"Hello?"

"Yeah, just like that."

"Hello. Hello," she said, as though testing the waters. After a moment she nodded. "Yeah, okay." She turned to him. "Hello. I think I've got it."

The humor that sparkled in her eyes was subtle but undeniable. "The job is yours."

She smiled, the first time he'd seen her smile all morning, and something went tight in his chest.

She turned away, glancing out the window as they made their way down Main Street. If he had any regrets, any misgivings, it was too late now. He'd had one opportunity after another to distance himself from her and he'd blown past every one. Maybe it was time for him to stop whining and accept some responsibility, accept the fact that for whatever reason, he was compelled to help this woman.

Maybe she was right, maybe he was a nice guy.

"Thank you, Sheriff."

He glanced at her, ready to say something amusingly sarcastic, but when he saw the look on her face, the words died on his lips. "You don't need to thank me."

"Yes, I do," she said, turning to look at him. "I don't know if I can tell you what it feels like, not having anything—no clothes, no money, no place to go. It's more than just frightening, it's…almost demoralizing." She stopped and drew in a deep breath, rubbing her palms slowly across her denim-covered thighs. ''Thank you for giving me a place, giving me something to do.''

She turned away again.

He wasn't sure what to say, wasn't even sure if he needed to say anything at all. He could empathize, but the path she walked was a lonely one.

When they reached the end of Main Street, Joe turned the Jeep onto the highway, picking up speed as they headed out the open road. It wouldn't be long before they reached Wheeler Road, the narrow, two-lane road that headed toward the ranch.

''It must get pretty quiet out here at night,'' Rain said after a while.

Joe couldn't be sure if there was an uneasiness in her voice, or just the normal awkwardness of small talk. ''You get used to it. And the desert has its own sounds—crickets and owls and an occasional coyote or two. They can get howling at the moon and make a terrible racket—''

''Coyotes,'' she said, sitting up so fast the seat belt nearly strangled her. She turned to him, him, her eyes wide with excitement. ''Coyotes. I remember hearing coyotes.''

''You mean, that night—''

''Yes! Yes!'' she said excitedly, interrupting him again. ''That night in the desert. I heard coyotes.'' She collapsed back against the seat. ''I remember hearing them howling.''

Joe's gaze darted back and forth from her to the highway. ''Was this when you were walking? While it was raining?''

Her smiled faded and she shook her head. ''No, it wasn't raining. It was dark, I can't...'' She let out a groan, pounding a fist against her forehead. "I don't know, I can't remember. But I heard them—I remember that. I heard them." She sat back up and turned to him again. "Do you think this means something? I mean, maybe I'm starting to bring something back." She squeezed her eyes tight. "Oh, God, wouldn't that be wonderful? If it could happen just like that, if it just came back."

It was easy to see what the recollection had done for her, how it had sent her hopes soaring only to leave her frustrated and stymied when she'd hit another brick wall. This is what Cruz had warned them about. The memory had just been there, popping into her head without any prompting—forcing it had done no good at all.

In the overall picture of things, what she had remembered did little to help solve the mystery of her past, but it had revealed something important to him. She must have been in the desert for a while. Coyotes didn't howl in the rain so she had to have been there since before the storm.

"That would be something," he said, purposely keeping his tone low-key and even. Could it happen that quickly? Could everything come back and the puzzle be solved as simply as that? "Just remember what Cruz said. You can't try to force it. It will happen when it happens."

"I know, I know," she said, drawing a deep, cleansing breath and resting a hand on her chest. "I shouldn't get excited, I shouldn't try to force it. But it was such a strange thing. I mean, suddenly it was just there—as clear as a bell. You mentioned coyotes and bam! I remember hearing the sound of them howling in the distance."

Joe braked carefully, turning from the highway and onto Wheeler Road. "You said it was dark."

She turned back, a deep furrow forming between her brows as she frowned. "I...I don't know. I think so— that is, it must have been." She looked away, her voice turning thoughtful. "I remember what a lonely sound that was—those coyotes howling." She gave her head another shake, turning back to him and smiling. "But at least I remembered something. I can't tell you what that means to me."

Her smile was so brilliant it very nearly took his breath. "It's a step in the right direction."

They rode the rest of the way in silence. Reaching the entrance to the narrow, twisting drive to his house, he slowed the Jeep.

"Is that it up there? That stand of trees?" she asked, sitting up in the seat once more.

"That's it," he replied, turning on the drive and picking up speed again. "Almost there."

"It looks so green—not like the desert," she said, peering through the window.

"There's an underground spring and a well."

"Carrie said you raise horses. Mustangs?"

"That's right. My pride and joy." He carefully steered around a big pothole in the road made bigger by the recent rain. "I'm going to breed the best, but that's a ways off yet. We're a pretty small operation now."

"Sounds exciting."

He shot her a skeptical glance. "Hardly exciting. Just a lot of hard work."

"But what a dream," she commented, catching sight of the house as he pulled the truck to a stop. "How lucky you are to build something like that together."

"Together?" Confused, he turned to her. But she already had the door open and was stepping out onto the drive. "Hey wait…Rain. Together? What—"

The slam of the door abruptly cut him off. Yanking the keys from the ignition, he climbed out of the SUV.

"Rain, what did you mean—"

"How lovely," she said, cutting him off.

Joe looked up at his two-story house with its steep roof, twin dormers and wraparound porch and couldn't deny the swell of pride. How different her reaction was in comparison to Karen's when she'd first seen the house. All she'd been able to do was complain about the dusty drive and how old and run-down the place had looked.

"It looks so different from the houses in town," she continued as he came around the vehicle.

In an area where low-slung ranch houses and adobe and tile prevailed, the pointed roof and stained-glass windows did make his house an anomaly in the desert, which was probably what drew him to it in the first place.

"The story is the original owner built the place for his new bride as a wedding present," he explained.

"Really?" She shaded her eyes from the sun, looking up at the weather vane perched at the top of the pointed roof. "Quite a wedding present I'd say."

"Apparently she had grown up in Boston and he'd felt so badly about taking her away from her family, he'd had the house built to look exactly like her family's home," he continued. Although he'd told the story a number of times to those interested enough to ask, this time it seemed to have new meaning to him. He found himself thinking about the new bed linens he'd purchased with Rain in mind and how he'd tried to pick out something he'd thought she might like, something he thought would make her feel comfortable. "He'd hoped it would make her feel more at home, help her not feel so lonesome living way out here."

"How romantic, and how thoughtful," she said in a quiet voice. Turning, she looked up at him. "Did it work?"

"From what I understand, they raised six kids in this house," he said, shrugging one shoulder. "I think it would be safe to say that it did."

"A happy ending," she said, her face brightening with a smile. "I think I like that."

Joe opened the back door and pulled out the brown paper bag Carrie had packed for her. "From what I understand, after about forty years here, they moved up to Alaska. One of their kids worked for an oil company up there." He slammed the door closed. "I know the place sat empty for a long time—seven, eight years—before I came along. It got pretty run-down, especially the stables."

"How long have you been here?"

"About six years. I'd known about the place for a long time." He gestured to the porch, following as she started toward it. "I grew up on the reservation just south of here. When I found out the place was vacant, I made some inquiries, found out it was for sale and put a down payment on it while I was still in the navy. Moved in after my discharge and have been trying to do repairs and improvements ever since. And like I said, there's still a lot to do."

"I think it looks great and it's obviously a great place to raise a family." When she reached the porch steps she stopped. "And Sheriff, before we go inside,

I just want to say again how much I appreciate your opening up your home to me. It is incredibly generous of you both...."

"Both?"

"...and someday I hope to repay both you and your wife for everything you've—"

"Whoa, whoa, whoa," he said, bringing up a hand and stopping her. "My wife?"

Chapter 6

Rain pulled the brush and comb from the brown paper bag and set them down on the bathroom counter beside the toothbrush, toothpaste and small bottles of shampoo and lotion. Except for the clothes awaiting analysis in a state crime lab somewhere in Carson City, the small row of toiletries were all the possessions she had.

He had left her alone to "unpack," which she could have done a hundred times over in the last several minutes. Still, she had appreciated the moment to herself, was grateful for some time alone to try to regain her composure.

Carefully folding the bag into a neat square, she looked around for a place to store it, deciding instead to toss it into the waste basket beside the counter. After arranging the articles on the shelf of the medicine cabinet, she closed the door and looked at herself in the mirror. She didn't know the name of the woman look-

ing back at her, but it was familiar—it was the face of
a woman flushed with excitement and smiling.

"Stop it," she demanded of the reflection. But as
though to mock her, the smile only widened and turned
sheepish.

There was no wife. It wasn't just a fact, it was a
revelation. There was no Mrs. Sheriff Mountain, no
lady of the house—not anymore, anyway. What Carrie
had neglected to add when she'd talked about Joe's
wife was that the lady was now the *ex*-Mrs. Mountain.

Hallelujah!

"Stop it!" she demanded again.

She turned around, leaning back against the pedestal
sink. Maybe she couldn't stop smiling, but she didn't
have to stand there and look at the sappy grin. And it
was sappy—sappy and ridiculous and completely un-
called for. So why couldn't she stop?

It had nothing to do with her. The sheriff's marital
status was of no concern to her. She had no business
having an opinion about it one way or the other—and
especially given the circumstances. She barely knew
the man, barely knew herself.

Why was she focusing so much on whether he was
married or not? He'd been nice to her, that was all. No
sense making more out of it than it was. It was important to keep perspective in all of this, to remind
herself that he was a stranger who had extended a hand
to her in a time of need.

She turned around and looked at herself in the mirror
again. "All right, that's enough," she snapped at the
silly woman grinning back at her. Forcing the muscles
in her face to relax, she squared her shoulders. "You're
going to straighten up and pull yourself together." She

pointed a warning finger. "Or it's the principal's office for you."

Suddenly something vibrated through her, something like a chill that had her bolting to attention. But before she had a chance to think about it, before she could even react, it was gone.

"What the hell?" she murmured to the reflection. "What was that?" But the infuriating woman in the mirror only stared back, her expression blank. "Well, enough of this." She inhaled, pulling deep, cleansing breaths into her lungs. "You get out there and take care of business." She started to turn away, then glanced back. "And just remember to keep perspective and don't let that imagination of yours go running amok, got it?"

With her resolve intact, and her composure, she darted out the bathroom, down the hall and into the bedroom, closing the door behind her. Leaning back against the smooth, solid oak, she looked around the room.

The house had five bedrooms and she couldn't help feeling pleased that Sheriff Mountain had chosen this one for her. She couldn't remember what her life had been like before, didn't know if she'd liked austere, empty spaces or had preferred to surround herself with color and form, but it didn't matter anyway. The important thing was, she liked what she saw now.

It wasn't a huge room, but it was filled with sunlight. A small window seat filled the space made by the dormer, looking out over the front drive and the stables beyond. The four-poster bed was small but sat high off the ground and the antique-lace-trimmed comforter and pillow shams looked crisp and clean and inviting. A nightstand with a small lamp was beside the bed and a highboy stood along the wall opposite it—inside which she found a few additional articles of clothing.

There was so little for her to draw from, so few experiences she'd had. With her past erased, her life had been reduced to only what she had known in the past several days. There had been no sunshine and laughter for her, no comfort and security. Yet something instinctive had her responding to the room and to the house. To one whose life had only known darkness and cold, it was a warm and wonderful place and she found herself rejoicing in it.

"Rain?"

The knock on the door behind her had her jumping.

"Yes?" Turning around she cracked the door open.

"I—I thought you might be hungry," Joe said, peaking awkwardly through the tiny open space. "I thought I'd fix us some sandwiches, if you'd like."

"Uh, yes," she stammered, opening the door wide. Something rumbled in her stomach at the mention of food. She thought about the bowl of oatmeal and two slices of toast she'd left untouched on her breakfast tray this morning. She'd been too nervous to eat then, but her appetite had definitely returned. "That sounds wonderful, thank you."

"I'll just go get things started," he said, taking several steps backward. "Whenever you're ready, you can come down."

"I'm ready," she said, stepping into the hallway. "I can help."

"Rule of the house," he said, stopping her. "I always fix the first meal. And sandwiches are something I can handle no matter what Cruz says."

Rain loved Joe Mountain's kitchen the moment she stepped into it. Sunlight poured in through the greenhouse window above the sink, and white ceramic tiles covered the wide expanse of kitchen counters. A round oak table sat in the bay window breakfast nook in front of an old-fashioned potbellied stove.

Lunch was a fairly simple affair of cold cuts, chips and sodas, yet Rain couldn't remember having tasted anything so heavenly. Not even that first meal in the hospital when she had rediscovered what it was to be hungry, had anything tasted quite as wonderful as her ham-and-cheese sandwich.

"That was delicious," she said, popping the last corner of sandwich into her mouth and pulling another handful of chips from the bag on the table.

Joe leaned back in his chair, watching as she popped several chips into her mouth. "Would you like another sandwich?"

She glanced down at her empty plate, then to his and felt her cheeks flush red. She'd all but inhaled her sandwich while he'd barely taken two bites of his.

"Uh, no," she said, shaking her head. "No, I'm fine. That was plenty."

"You sure?"

She didn't want to impose, but the truth was, she was hungry. "You sure you don't mind?"

He smiled as he leaned forward and reached for her plate, pushing himself away from the table. "I don't mind at all."

"I guess maybe they should have warned you," she told him as he walked to the kitchen counter.

"Warned me?"

She nodded. "My memory might not be very good, but apparently there is nothing wrong with my appetite."

"Is that right?"

"Right."

"Then I think we'll probably get along just fine," he said as he worked. "I find it helps to have a healthy appetite when you're eating meals I fix." He put the finished sandwich on her plate and carried it back to her. "Sort of helps things go down a little easier."

"Thank you," she said as he set the plate down in front of her. Picking up the sandwich, she took a healthy bite. "Carrie said almost the same thing when I woke up starving in the hospital. I liked that food, too."

"You liked the hospital food?" He laughed. "You really aren't fussy about what you eat, are you?" He watched her chew and take another bite and smiled. "Is there something especially you're hungry for? Something you'd like me to pick up at the store?"

She swallowed and thought for a moment. "No, I seem to like pretty much anything that's put in front of me."

"Well, that's convenient," he said, picking up his unfinished sandwich and taking another bite. "And makes meal planning a lot easier."

"What kind of food do you like?" she asked, reaching for more chips. "Italian? Mexican? Chinese? Or are you a meat-and-potatoes man?"

"I like just about everything," he said, taking a sip from his soda can. "As a kid I couldn't afford to be fussy. Things could get rough on the reservation and there were times we were just lucky to have a meal." He reached for a chip, popping it into his mouth. "But in the navy I was in a lot of different places and had a chance to try a lot of different things. I ate sushi while I was in Japan and calimari in Italy. But my tastes still run pretty simple. Nothing beats a good steak as far as I'm concerned.''

"A New York, rare, with crumbled blue cheese on top?''

His eyes widened. "That's my favorite. You, too?''

She swallowed the last of her sandwich and shrugged. "I don't know, but it sounds good.'' She reached for her soda can, taking a drink. "I wonder if that counts as a recollection.''

They looked at one another, each of them holding a can of soda, and shook their heads together.

"Nah,'' they said in unison.

"Feel up to a little tour?'' Joe asked once they'd both finished their lunches. "I thought you might like to see the stables.''

"I'd love to,'' Rain said, reaching for their empty plates and carrying them to the sink. "It'll just take me a minute to clean up here.''

"Leave those,'' he said, crushing their empty soda cans with one squeeze and tossing them into a plastic bucket beside the back door. "I'll take care of them later.''

"I don't mind,'' she insisted, rinsing the plates and slipping them into the dishwasher. "I want to help.'' She put the mayonnaise and mustard back into the refrigerator and returned the loaf of bread to the pantry. "Makes me feel useful.'' she added, but there was something about the neatly lined shelves of canned goods and staples that caught her attention.

"Find something interesting in there?''

She jumped and turned to Joe at the door of the pantry. "I don't know,'' she said honestly, glancing back at the shelves of food. "Something…'' She shook her head and started for the door. "I get these funny feelings about things sometimes, like maybe they're familiar, I don't know. Maybe I work in a food store or something—you know, restock shelves?'' She walked out of the pantry, closing the door behind her. ''That or maybe I just like to hang out in supermarkets.''

''Supermarket freak, huh? Makes sense with that appetite of yours,'' he concluded. ''Just remind me never to take you grocery shopping.''

They quickly finished up the kitchen and headed outside for the stables. She couldn't help noticing what a different man Joe Mountain was in his home surroundings. He seemed more relaxed, more comfortable and more willing to let his guard down. There had been something in his eyes when he'd talked about growing up on the reservation, something sad and poignant.

She suspected he wasn't comfortable talking about himself, wouldn't intentionally give up a lot of information, yet he'd managed to impart a few details. She'd learned his life on the reservation hadn't been an easy one and she'd learned he'd joined the navy and traveled the world. Of course, there were a million questions she had about both subjects but she would refrain from asking. He'd opened up his home to her; that wasn't an invitation to open up his entire life.

''And this is Sycamore,'' he said, petting the narrow face of the two-year-old mare. ''She's my pride and joy.''

''She's beautiful,'' Rain said, hesitantly reaching up and giving the horse a small pat on the nose.

He had given her a quick tour of the ranch. And while it was obvious he loved his unusual house, there was no doubt that his heart belonged to the stables and the horses he housed there.

"She is that," he agreed, reaching into his pocket and pulling out a cube of sugar. Spotting the treat, the horse nudged him with her nose. "But just like every woman, she requires a little special attention from time to time." He offered her the sugar cube, scratching her under the chin as she chewed. "Don't you, little girl?"

"Have you always been interested in horses?"

"Pretty much," he said, stepping back to open the stall door. "My dad had a couple of horses." He took a hand brush down from a hook on the wall and slipped his fingers through the leather strap along the back. "Of course, they were just old plow horses. We never had an animal like this." He brushed the horse's shiny coat with broad strokes. "My dad would have loved this beauty."

"He's gone, your father?"

Joe nodded. "Died while I was in the navy."

There was something strained and tight in his voice, something that made her think there was a lot more to the story than he was saying. He took several more swipes with the brush, then turned to her.

"Want to try?"

Rain looked at the brush, then at the huge animal. She should have been afraid, should have shrank back against the stall door but something told her she had nothing to fear.

"Come on," he urged. "She's a sweetheart. She won't hurt you."

"Maybe not," she said as she gingerly stepped into the stall and slipped her hand through the strap of the brush. "But she's going to need a little time to get used to me."

"Nice gentle strokes," he instructed in a soothing

voice as he carefully guided her hand over the horse's coat.

As though sensing the touch of a stranger, the horse reacted. Turning its head, it glared back at Rain and snorted.

"Sycamore, be polite," Joe scolded, moving Rain's hand over the animal again. Leaning close, he whispered into her ear. "Just keep stroking. Don't let her bully you."

Rain was nervous, but it had nothing to do with being in such close proximity to the spirited animal. With Joe standing behind her, with his hand on hers and his body brushing hers it was all she could to think about the horse at all.

"Now you're getting the hang of it," he praised as she slid the brush along the satiny hide. "See how relaxed she's become?"

Rain drew in a shaky breath. "I'm glad one of us is."

"You're doing fine," he insisted, stepping back a few paces.

With him not so close, she relaxed a little, too. She realized he had mistaken her uneasiness for nerves about the horse, but that was just fine with her. He didn't need to know having him so close had made her jumpier than Sycamore's nervous snorts. "So how do I make sure she doesn't just decide she's had enough and puts a hoof down on one of my toes?"

"You keep your eyes open," he advised in a wry tone. "And be prepared to move out of the way—as fast as you can."

Despite her uneasiness, she had to laugh. She continued brushing Sycamore, stroking with more assurance the more relaxed she became. The horse had become almost sedate and Rain had to admit there was something soothing and serene about the activity. The horse's coat shone like satin and felt silky against the palm of her hand.

"You do this every day?"

He nodded, folding his arms across his chest as he leaned back against the closed stall door. "Several times during the day when I can. Horses take work and I don't always have enough time myself so I have someone who helps me. He's here every day—Charlie Evers, I'll introduce you."

She nodded as she continued to brush. She wasn't sure how she'd done it, but somehow she'd managed to brush her way around to the other side of the horse.

"Labor of love?" she asked, looking at him from over the top of the horse.

"Absolutely," he admitted. "But you've got to love it to be in the horse business. Otherwise why bother?" He pushed himself away from the door and walked around Sycamore to where Rain stood. "And I think you've managed to spoil her enough for one day."

"I don't know about spoiling her," she said, slipping her hand free from the strap. Reaching up, she even felt bold enough to give the horse a pat on the nose. "But she does seem a little more used to me now."

"Oh, I think it's safe to say she's got your number," he commented, taking the brush from her and returning it to the hook on the wall. "Just notice the difference in the way she greets you next time you come in."

He opened the stall door, holding it open for her and securing the lock once she'd passed through.

"You know how back in the kitchen I said something in the pantry seemed familiar?'' she asked, stopping as they started out of the stables.

"Yeah."

"I have that same feeling about horses."

"Oh, yeah? You think you might have worked around horses?"

"I don't know about that," she admitted, "but I do know I must have forgotten one very important thing."

"Oh, yeah? What would that be?"

With a purposeful move, she looked down at her borrowed tennis shoe. "Watch where you're walking."

"Oh, my, now that's not a pretty sight."

"Not a pretty sight at all," she agreed with a sigh, not knowing whether she wanted to laugh or burst into tears.

He glanced down at her shoes again, then slowly nodded his head. "Yup, I think you're right." Taking her hand, he led her back into the stable. "When it comes to horses, you just might be a greenhorn."

"How you doing in here? Feel okay?"

Rain looked up from the file cabinet. "I feel great."

Joe couldn't help thinking that she looked pretty great, too, but he refrained from voicing that observation. "Not too tired?"

She shook her head as she pushed in one file drawer and pulled out another. "Not at all. I'm just about through here."

"You're kidding." Joe glanced at the top of the file cabinet where a huge stack of folders had accumulated over the last week, surprised to see its size had shrunk considerably. She was supposed to just answer the phones, but somehow she'd managed to get most of their filing done, too. "You're doing too much. Maybe you should sit down and rest for a little while."

"What? Don't be silly, I'm fine. This is nothing," she said, waving off his concern. "It's just a little filing—basic ABCs."

"But it's not necessary for you to get it all done today. Cruz warned you not to overdo."

"Believe me, this is not overdoing," she assured him, reaching for another file from the diminishing stack. "In fact, I'm enjoying myself."

"You enjoying filing?" he commented skeptically. "I find that hard to believe."

She looked up at him and grinned. "Well, believe it. I enjoy it. Who knows, maybe I'm a secretary or a librarian."

Joe found that he was grinning back and felt foolish. Clearing his throat, he forced the smile from his face. "How about a cup of coffee then? Could I bring you a cup?"

"You're the boss," she pointed out. "Shouldn't I be the one asking you that?"

He shrugged. "It's your first day. I thought I'd go easy on you."

She laughed. "Well, I appreciate it. And no, you don't need to bring me any coffee. I just finished one and I had two cups at breakfast in case you didn't notice."

He'd noticed. In fact, he'd noticed a lot of things about her in the twenty-four hours since she'd come to stay with him. They'd made it through their first day—and first night—under the same roof but it hadn't been without a few awkward moments.

After he'd given her the Cook's tour of the house and stables, she'd gone to her room and pretty much kept to herself for the rest of the day. She'd come downstairs only once, at his prompting, to join him for a light dinner only to beat it back to her room where she'd stayed until this morning.

"Apparently I'm a coffee drinker," she continued, slipping a folder into the file drawer and pushing it closed. "Or at least I am now. Would you like me to bring you a cup, though? I just made a fresh pot about ten minutes ago."

"You made coffee?" His voice perked up.

The smile faded from her lips. "The pot was empty. I hope that was all right."

"Are you kidding? Have you tasted Ryan's coffee?"

"Actually—" she leaned close, her voice lowering "—that's why I made the fresh pot. It was a little..."

"Deadly? Lethal? Dangerous?" he suggested for her.

She laughed as she reached for another folder. "I was thinking *strong*."

"Felony *strong,* maybe," he corrected dryly. He watched as she pulled out another drawer and filed the folder inside. "You sure you don't want to sit down and rest for a while?"

"I'm sure."

"You're not overdoing?"

She gave him a purposeful look. "ABCs, Sheriff. ABCs."

"All right, all right, ABCs, I got it." He laughed, holding his hands up in surrender. He turned and stepped into the corridor. "When you're through with the alphabet, give me a shout. I'll take you next door to the diner and buy you some lunch."

"I just might take you up on that," she said, reaching for another folder.

"But then you're going home," he said through the open doorway. "Half a day is enough to start out with."

"Like I said before, you're the boss," she called after him as she pulled open another drawer.

Joe walked down the corridor, following the aroma of fresh-brewed coffee. He was grateful for the easy rapport between them, relieved the awkwardness from last night and this morning hadn't followed them in.

He may not know much about her, but already he could vouch for the fact that she was a hard worker. She hadn't been shy or timid about helping out. After he'd shown her around the office, she'd delved into that mountain of filing with determination and zeal.

She'd surprised him when she'd joined him for a hurried breakfast this morning. He hadn't really expected her to come into the office with him. He'd thought she would want at least a day or two to acclimatize herself a little to the world outside or to rest up and gather her strength. Yet there she'd been bright and early this morning, waiting for him in the kitchen, dressed in one of Karen's old dresses and brewing up a pot of coffee.

"Coffee," he murmured aloud, breathing in the delicious aroma. But the as he rounded the corner into the break room, he came to a dead stop. "Wh-what are you doing?" he demanded.

Ryan stopped and slowly turned around, his brow arched in surprise. "What? I'm just getting some coffee. Why?"

Joe's gaze bounced from Ryan's thermos on the counter to the empty coffeepot in his hand.

Deflated, he shook his head. "No reason."

He watched as Ryan took the empty pot and filled it with fresh water.

"Now what are you doing?"

Ryan stopped and slowly turned around, giving him a skeptical look. "I was going to make another pot of coffee."

The thought of Ryan's ultralethal brews had his stomach rolling over.

"No!" he said, jumping forward. "No, that's okay. You head off for patrol."

Ryan gave him another skeptical look. "You okay, Joe?"

"I'm fine," Joe said, feeling a little foolish.

"How's Rain doing?" Ryan asked, reaching for the cap of his thermos and screwing it on tight.

"Okay, I think," he said, picking up a paper filter and slipping it inside the plastic holder of the coffee-maker. "You're not going to believe it, but she's practically done with the filing."

Ryan looked up, eyebrows slowly raising. "And she hasn't gone stark raving mad or pulled out her hair yet?"

Joe smiled. "No, but I'm not going to take any chances. I'm taking her back out to the ranch after lunch."

"She feeling okay?"

Ryan's look of concern was so genuine Joe couldn't help wondering if there was something about the woman that brought out a common reaction from all who met her. Maybe his feelings weren't so unusual, maybe she brought out feelings of protection in everyone.

"I think so, but Cruz says she needs to take it

slow.'' Joe poured the coffee grounds into the filter. ''She's been through a lot.''

''Yeah, you're right and that's just what we've managed to put together,'' Ryan commented, picking up his thermos. ''God only knows how long she was out in that desert—or what happened.''

Joe frowned. Somebody besides God knew and one way or another he was going to find out who that was.

''Was it your idea to have her help out?''

Joe immediately felt his defenses go up. ''You got a problem with her being here?''

Ryan snorted out a laugh. ''No, why would I?''

''Then what difference does it make whose idea it was?''

Ryan regarded him for a moment. ''It doesn't. I was curious, that's all. I'm a cop, being curious is what I do for a living.''

Joe knew he was making too much of Ryan's interest and felt embarrassed. ''It was my idea. I thought it might help if she kept herself busy and she's got this thing...'' He shrugged, letting his words drift.

''Thing?'' Ryan prompted.

Joe looked up and shrugged again. ''She needs to feel useful. The thought of just sitting around and doing nothing bothers her. She wants to keep busy.''

''Well, we've got enough around here to keep her busy for a while,'' Ryan commented dryly. ''Damn shame, though.''

Joe looked up.

''Not being able to remember,'' Ryan explained, looking up at Joe. ''She's a nice woman. There's someone out there—family, kids—somebody is missing her.''

Chapter 7

"Sal, this is Rain and she would like you to bring her the biggest lunch plate special you've got."

The voluminous waitress peered over the top of her rhinestone-framed glasses, surveying Rain with a curious eye. "Rain, huh? Yeah, I've heard about you, the woman from the desert. Nice to meet you, honey."

Rain felt heat crawl up her neck and deposit into her cheeks. Suddenly she felt every eye in the place on her.

"Nice..." She cleared her throat, feeling her face flame brighter. "Nice to meet you, too."

Joe reached for a trifolded menu from behind the napkin dispenser and opened it up. "So what's looking good today?"

Sal arched a painted brow and reached for the pencil that pierced her almost perfect beehive hairdo. "You say you're hungry, huh? Well, Walt don't skimp on the meat loaf sandwich. Think you could handle that, sweetie?''

''Sounds good,'' Rain confessed, hunger getting the best of her embarrassment just a little. ''I am pretty hungry.''

''Well you won't be after this, hon,'' Sal assured her, pulling a tablet from her apron and scrawling across it. ''And how about you, sweet stuff?'' she asked, turning to Joe. ''Gonna let the little lady get one up on you?''

''Walt's meat loaf sandwich you say.'' Joe considered this for a moment, running a perusing eye over the menu, then shot a challenging look at Rain. ''Oh, I think I can give her a run for her money.'' He glanced back up at Sal. ''Bring me the meat loaf, too.''

Sal slapped the tablet closed and tucked the pencil back into her hair. ''Two meat loaf sandwich specials coming up.''

''This place is great,'' Rain said as the waitress made her way through the crowded diner and around the counter. ''Do you eat here often?''

''Couple times a week.'' Joe leaned back and patted his stomach. ''I couldn't do any more than that.''

Rain watched the interplay of the other patrons. The atmosphere was loud and chaotic with the noon rush lunch crowd. Even though she felt like everyone was staring at her, the truth of the matter was everyone was too busy eating to take much notice of her. Still, she felt conspicuous sitting there dressed in another woman's clothes. Did everyone know about her? Did they all know she was the woman with no past?

''Busy place,'' she commented, turning to Joe. ''Food must be good.''

Joe nodded. "Nobody does greasy spoon better than Sal and Walt."

"Which one's Walt?"

"The guy in the Harley-Davidson T-shirt at the grill," he told her, lifting his chin in the general direction. "He learned to cook while he was in prison."

Rain's eyes widened. "Prison?"

Joe laughed at Rain's reaction. "Sentenced to fifteen years for armed robbery—served ten."

Rain turned and looked at the hulking man working behind the counter. "Oh, really."

"And as a matter of fact," he added, leaning forward and lowering his voice. "That's where he met Sal."

"What?" she gasped, turning back to him. "They met in prison?"

Joe nodded. "She was a guard."

"You're kidding."

His smile widened. "Don't you just love a happy ending?"

Rain sank back against the booth. "What a story."

Joe sat back, too. "We might not be the biggest community in the state, but we've got our share of colorful characters. Well, here comes our lunch now."

Rain looked down in wonder at the platter of food in front of her. To say she'd had a voracious hunger since she'd awakened in the hospital would be an understatement, but looking at the meat loaf sandwich lunch special, she suddenly wondered if she hadn't met her match.

Joe smiled. "If the plates were any larger, they'd have to use a crane to carry them to the tables."

"And another to lift their patrons out," Rain joked,

spearing a healthy wedge of meat loaf with her fork and popping it into her mouth.

Joe laughed. "Remind me to start a diet tomorrow."

Rain laughed, too. She'd had some reservations when Joe had suggested taking her to lunch, had felt a little reluctant about being out in public. Carrie had told her Mesa Ridge was a small town. Everyone had acknowledged Joe as he'd walked by and she didn't doubt they had all heard about her. Her story had been reported in the local newspaper and broadcast on the television news. She felt like a freak, like an outsider with no name, no past and no place to call home.

Of course, it hadn't helped either that she felt awkward dressed in clothes that obviously didn't fit right. As much as she appreciated Joe's kindness in providing her with clothes to wear, it bothered her that they were the hand-me-downs of his ex-wife. It was ungrateful, she knew, but she felt self-conscious and unattractive in them. She couldn't remember what her own clothes looked like, but she was fairly certain she wouldn't have chosen any like these. Karen Mountain's tastes ran to the bright, the tight and the gaudy, and the bright-pink flowered dress she had on now fit that criteria exactly.

"So tell me some more about Mesa Ridge," she said. "Any more eccentric types?"

"One or two," Joe said, scooping up a forkful of mashed potatoes. "I think there's something about the desert or the wide-open spaces that attract unusual people or those with checkered pasts."

"And sometimes even those with no pasts at all," she added in a quiet voice.

He paused, glancing at her from across the table.

"Sometimes," he acknowledged. "And sometimes it's a place people come to find their lives again."

There was something so soft in his voice, something so earnest in his expression it had her heart stumbling. "What about you, Sheriff Mountain? Is that why you came back to Mesa Ridge? To find your life again?"

Joe poked at his mashed potatoes. "Maybe. It seems that before I went into the navy, all I could think about was getting off the reservation, out of Mesa County and as far away from here as I could get."

"And yet you came back."

He shrugged and reached for his glass. "It's home. After knocking around the world for four or five years, I was ready to come home."

Rain felt a sudden lump of emotion in her throat. "I wonder if I'll ever find home again."

"When the time is right," he assured her.

They both turned back to their food, finishing their meal in silence. But despite the noise and pandemonium around them, the silence between them was thick and awkward.

"You managed to make a pretty good dent in that, honey," Sal said, pointing to the near-empty plate.

"Thank you," Rain said, sitting back and taking a deep breath. "But I may never eat again."

"So, you two ready for dessert?" Sal asked as began to stack the dirty dishes.

"Dessert?" Rain looked up at her as though she'd just made an off-color remark because the thought of putting another morsel of food into her mouth seemed offensive and wholly inappropriate.

"Hot apple pie, made fresh this morning." Sal turned to Joe. "How about you, Sheriff? If I'm not mistaken, I think that's your favorite."

"You're not mistaken, Sal, but I'm going to have to pass this time." He gave Rain an expectant look. "How about you? Up for a little pie?"

When Rain shook her head, Sal tore the bill from her tablet and set it face down on the table. "Well, it was nice meeting you, hon, and you two have a real nice afternoon, okay?"

The diner had emptied out considerably and Rain felt much less conspicuous as they walked out.

"About your doctor's appointment in the morning," Joe said as he started the engine of his four-wheel-drive SUV. "I thought if you were feeling up to it on the way back we'd swing by the area where you'd been wandering, maybe take a look around to see if it jogs anything. What do you think?"

Rain had to admit she'd been a little anxious about the appointment she had tomorrow with the specialist Cruz had arranged for her to see. She didn't look forward to delving into all those black areas in her memory, all those shadowy demons that haunted her sleep. It made her feel anxious and uneasy, but if that was what it took in order to get her life back, then it's what she would do. Still, she didn't look forward to it and took an irrational comfort in knowing Joe would be there with her.

"I think that would be fine," she said.

"And if it turns out you're too tired, we'll put it off for a few days."

Rain shook her head. "No, I'll be okay."

"Good."

They drove back to the ranch in silence, but it was a comfortable silence this time. Rain watched the arid landscape pass, thinking about the morning she'd spent in Joe's office and the lunch they'd shared together.

This was his world, the life he'd chosen and the place he'd chosen to be. What was it about this empty piece of the world, this small town and its singular inhabitants that made it home to him? And what was it about Joe Mountain's world that she found so inviting?

The aroma hit him the moment he stepped out of the truck, bringing him to a dead stop. Garlic, tomato, onion and...

He walked to the back stairs, inhaling deeply. Oregano? Climbing the steps to the door, he drew in another breath, feeling himself start to salivate. Oregano, definitely.

Slowly leaning forward, he peered through the open doorway.

"Please tell me you're hungry," Rain said, spotting him as he stepped into the kitchen.

Considering the size of the lunch he'd had, it surprised him to realize that he was. "What's all this?"

"I know how to cook," she announced through clouds of steam billowing up from the simmering pots on the stove. "I know how to cook a lot."

And cook was what she had done—in a big way.

He walked to the stove and began lifting lids and sampling dishes. "Chili con carne, spaghetti sauce, stuffed peppers?" Hardly believing the simmering feast before him, he turned to her. "What happened?"

She glanced up at him, looking overwhelmed and confused and her eyes glistened with tears. "It's awful, isn't it?"

"Awful?" Her helpless, vulnerable expression tugged at something in him and it was all he could do to stop himself from pulling her into his arms. "What do you mean awful? It all looks delicious."

"I don't know how it happened," she explained, her voice cracking with emotion. She reached for a towel and wiped her hands. "I mean, I just walked into the pantry to get a tea bag and I noticed the spices lined up on the shelf...the chili powder, the cumin, the oregano, the garlic, and the next thing I knew—" she twisted the towel in her hands "—all this." A tear slipped down her cheek. "I am so sorry."

"Sorry? Don't be silly," he insisted. "This is wonderful."

She sniffed. "Really?"

"Really," he said, reaching for a paper towel from the dispenser mounted on the pantry door and handing it to her. "Now blow."

She did as she was told. "You're not angry then?"

"Of course not," he said, looking at all the food again. He'd dropped her back at the ranch after lunch with strict instructions that she rest, but it was obvious she had defied his directive. "But this must have taken you hours."

She blew her nose again. "I don't know. What time is it?"

"Dinnertime," he said, picking up a spoon and sampling the spaghetti sauce. It was warm, rich and spicy. Picking up a fork, he pierced a meatball "I'm just wondering what army we're going to feed all this to."

In control now, she walked to the sink and washed her hands. "Maybe we could freeze some—and take hot lunches to work."

"With food like this around," Joe said, taking a bite of meatball. "I don't think I'll be seeing Sal for quite some time."

"Okay, so what do you want for dinner?" she asked, reaching for a package of dry pasta. "Spaghetti and meatballs? The chili? A stuffed pepper?"

Joe popped the rest of the meatball into his mouth. "Okay."

"Okay?"

"Yeah," he shrugged, walking to the cupboard and pulling out two plates. "Just what you said—spaghetti, chili and peppers."

"You want some of everything?"

He looked at her and shrugged. "Why not?"

She thought for a moment, then smiled and shrugged herself. "Yeah, why not." She pulled out a drawer and grabbed utensils enough for both of them. "And maybe I'm not the only one with a healthy appetite."

Dinner had been more than dinner, it had been a feast. Even though his eyes had been a bit bigger than his appetite, he'd still managed to eat enough to make himself miserable.

"Delicious," he announced, tossing down his fork when he couldn't hold another bite.

"Which?"

"Everything," he said simply. "You are one hell of a cook."

"It was so strange," she confessed, leaning back in her chair. "It wasn't as though I actually remembered anything. I mean, a recipe didn't flash in my mind—a pound of this, two tablespoons of that. I just sort of did it. Somehow I just knew." She reached for her glass of water, taking a sip. "I suppose that's something I should discuss with Dr. McGhan in the morning."

"Probably wouldn't be a bad idea," he said, pushing his chair back away from the table and rising to his feet. Gravity sent the food in his system to the very bottom of his stomach, and he groaned.

"Are you all right?"

"Fine," he insisted, giving his swollen tummy a gentle pat. "Just thinking about having a little antacid for dessert."

"I thought you said I was a good cook?"

Her mischievous smile was almost as devastating as that soft, vulnerable look of hers. "You are too good of a cook, so good that I'm miserable. And now the cook gets to rest," he announced as he began clearing the dishes from the table. "I'm cleaning up."

"But I can help—"

"Don't you dare," he warned as she started to reach for her plate. "You've done enough for one day—too much, in fact. The only thing you're going to do is relax."

"Well, I am a little tired," she admitted, sinking back into her chair.

"Cruz would have my hide if he knew how much you'd done today," he said, carrying an armload of dirty dishes to the sink. "You're suppose to be taking things slow."

"That's what I'm doing."

He turned and gave her a look. "I don't think working all morning and cooking all afternoon qualifies."

"Maybe not," she confessed. "But to be honest, it felt good. All I've done is rest. I just spent four days in the hospital. It felt good to do something for a change."

"Need I remind you that you were recuperating from a rather serious bump on the head?" he asked, purposely sounding sarcastic. "Not to mention exposure from one pretty nasty storm?"

"No, you don't need to remind me, thank you very much," she acknowledged with a saccharine smile. "But the doctor also gave me a clean bill of health—physically anyway." She closed her eyes and sighed. "And now I feel tired." Opening her eyes, she stopped him before he could say anything. "Deliciously tired which means I will sleep soundly tonight—no bad dreams."

"Well, why don't you take your *deliciously* tired self out onto the porch and relax while I finish up here? There should be a full moon out tonight."

"You sure you wouldn't like some—"

Holding up his hand, he gave her a killing look. "Don't even finish that sentence."

She held her hands up in surrender. "I wasn't going to say another word."

He watched as she walked out of the kitchen and through the dining room toward the front porch. She'd had a big day—too big, and he blamed himself for the signs of fatigue that darkened the tender skin beneath her eyes. Still, it had been wonderful to see her enthusiastic and excited about life. She'd been through so much, had seen and experienced the kind of fear no one should have to experience, the kind that was so devastating, so horrific that forgetting had been the only way to survive. If she'd gone a little overboard on her first day out, he would forgive her. She deserved it.

He quietly went about the job of cleaning up, the mundane chores making him forget about the discomfort of having eaten too much. He thought of the look on her face when he'd walked into the kitchen. She had looked confused and frightened and completely bewildered. Like an animal in the wilds, her instincts had taken command. He only hoped some of those instincts would resurface tomorrow in the desert and give him something concrete to go on.

"It's such a beautiful night," she said as he walked out on the porch after finishing in the kitchen. She was sitting on the top step, hugging her knees close to her chest and looking up at the sky. "I just saw a shooting star."

"Did you make a wish?"

She turned and looked up at him. "I did. Want to hear it?"

She looked beautiful sitting there, her skin looking like satin in the moonlight. The curl of desire that seared in his belly wasn't entirely unexpected. He was, after all, a man; and men wanted women, especially women who looked like her.

The only problem was, he wasn't just any man and she wasn't just any woman. She was a woman with no past, a woman who had lost who she was and he was the man who had to help her find her way again.

"Maybe you shouldn't. It might not come true."

"I'm not superstitious," she said, leaning her head back against the rail post.

"Oh, really."

She turned her head and looked up at him. "Not that I know of anyway."

"Okay then," he said, lowering himself on to the top step opposite her. "Tell me what you wished for."

She glanced back to the night sky. "I wished that I could feel every night the way I feel tonight."

Suddenly the desire simmering in his gut didn't seem so innocent. "And how is that?"

"Warm, safe, hopeful," she murmured.

"And full."

She laughed, turning to look at him again. "Very full." Her smile slowly faded. "And especially safe. I don't ever want to be afraid of the night again."

Joe sat up long after Rain had gone to bed trying to convince himself that what she had said meant nothing to him. Why shouldn't she feel safe? She wasn't in the desert any longer and whoever or whatever it was that had left her out there was no longer in her life. She was in a place and around people who were not threatening to her, who only wanted to help and restore her to the life she'd been taken from. She had every right to feel safe. It was not only understandable, it was reasonable and to be expected.

So why did her affirmation touch him so? Why was he having trouble breathing just thinking how she had looked sitting there looking up at him?

"Too close," he murmured aloud. He was getting too close, too involved and it had to... "Stop—right here, right now."

He was determined. Whatever game he was playing with himself, whatever fantasy or delusion that overtook him every time he looked at the woman was going to end—it had to. It wasn't just a matter of keeping perspective, of reminding himself what he had to do as opposed to what he wanted to do. It was a matter of him doing his job and not allowing himself to be distracted.

It had been almost a week since she'd walked out of the desert and into his life. He'd spent days poring over missing persons reports and checking criminal databases and coming up with nothing. There had been a roadblock or a brick wall at the end of every lead they'd followed. He had no better idea now what had happened than he had that dark, stormy night, no clue as to who she was or where she belonged.

She was doing her best to adjust, healing from her physical injuries and grasping at what bits and pieces of her past she could. It was up to him to keep himself on target, to remember the job he had to do and not get distracted by moonlight.

He wasn't a man given to fantasies and yet it seemed he'd had his share since she'd come into his life. He didn't blame her; the fault was with him. She wasn't forcing herself into his thoughts or into his life—that had all been his own doing. No one had held a gun to his head. It had been his choice to take her in, his choice to offer her work at the sheriff's office, his choice to notice just how beautiful she looked in the moonlight.

"Right here, right now," he whispered, reminding himself again. The fantasies, the delusions, the curl of hunger and need. They all ended. "Right here, right now."

The gun was in his hand even before his eyes were open. He sat up, his heart pounding, the silence almost deafening as he strained to listen.

Air entered and exited his lungs, making his breath sound like a freight train in his ears, and so he held it.

It wasn't as though the sound had been loud, because it hadn't. It had been a faint, barely audible disturbance, yet one he'd been aware of immediately. It had been out of place, different and had broken the rhythm of the night, interfered with the unique sound of the house just as a train whistle shatters the silence of the countryside it passes through.

He sat frozen, feeling every taut, tight muscle in his

body, but there was nothing in the darkness now—
nothing but the normal sounds of the house and the
pulsing of his own heart in his ears. Whatever had
awakened him was gone now and he let out his breath
in one long, slow sigh. Easing his grip on the gun, he
turned to slip it back into the holster that hung from
the bedpost when he heard it again.

He didn't wait to listen this time. He was on his feet
and to the door of his bedroom before he even took
another breath.

Again it wasn't loud, nothing as dramatic or startling. It wasn't a scream, couldn't even be considered
a cry, but still there was something soulful and pleading about the sound, like the last gasps of an animal
caught in a trap.

Opening the bedroom door, he stepped out into the
hallway. Immediately the sound not only became
louder, but clearer as well. He could tell now that it
wasn't a gasp, nor was it a cry. It was more tormented
than that, more of an anguished, sorrowful moan.

Slowly starting down the corridor, it didn't take long
for him to determine where the sound was coming
from. It came from the other end of the hallway, from
Rain's room. She was having a nightmare.

The bedroom, when he opened the door, was flooded
with the white, silvery light of the moon.

"No," she groaned, her head turning back and forth
on the pillow. "Is it Logan? No."

There it was again. Logan. The sound of her voice
when she said the name sent a chill running down his
spine. She was terrified.

"Rain," he whispered, walking to the bed. Kneeling
down, he carefully set the gun on the carpet next to
him. "Rain, you're dreaming."

"It's not Logan, not Logan," she mumbled. "Not Logan."

"Wake up, Rain," he urged, reaching for her and giving each shoulder a gentle shake. "Come on, it's Joe. Wake up."

Her eyes shot open and for a moment he wondered who it was she was seeing when she looked at him because it was obvious she wasn't seeing him.

"It's me, it's Joe. You're awake now."

"J-Joe?" she stammered, recognition coming to her eyes.

"It's okay," he assured her, pulling her close and feeling the pounding of her heart pulsing wildly against him. "You're safe."

"Safe," she murmured, her breath coming in jagged, uneven gasps. "Safe."

Chapter 8

"Logan."

Rain leaned forward and nodded. "Do you think it means something?"

Michael McGhan reached for the glasses perched on his head and slid them into place at the bridge of his nose. "It undoubtedly means something," he admitted, picking up the chart from his desk again. "We just don't know what that is."

Rain watched as he read through the file again, feeling herself growing more agitated and more anxious the longer he read. She wasn't sure why she felt so uneasy. It wasn't as though the doctor had been unpleasant or the appointment was going badly. On the contrary. She found Dr. McGhan to be a kind, compassionate man with a warm, pleasant personality and professional "bedside manner." She'd had no difficulty in talking to him. He listened carefully to what she said to him and his questions had been insightful and thought provoking.

So why was she becoming so annoyed? Why did his careful study of her file make her feel resentful and angry?

After a brief introduction, the doctor had reviewed and discussed with her all the medical records Dr. Martinez had forwarded to him, made a brief diagnosis and outlined a course of treatment. She'd felt comfortable, optimistic even, about firming up the weekly sessions he recommended and discussing the various forms of therapy he offered. However, when he began asking her about her dreams—about Logan—she'd felt herself tightening up.

She thought about last night, about the nightmare and about waking up in Joe Mountain's embrace. It hadn't been the first time he'd been there when she'd awakened from a nightmare, but it had been the first time she'd found herself in his arms.

Of course, she'd been too upset, too frightened to question why he'd been there, or why it had meant so much. She'd just been grateful. His arms had felt strong and secure around her and in them, she had forgotten about the fear and the terror. She had forgotten about Logan. He had held her for a long time, held her until she could sleep again and falling asleep in his arms had been the best rest she'd ever had.

"Logan," Dr. McGhan said again. Lowering the file, he pushed his glasses back up onto his forehead. "Nothing else, just Logan, right?"

"Just…just Logan," Rain mumbled, opening up her hands and rubbing her damp palms across the fabric of her skirt. She shifted uneasily in the chair. "Everything always seems so mixed up, so confusing."

"In the dream," he said, leaning back in his chair and tenting his fingers together. "And you can't tell from the dreams if Logan is a person or a place."

"Sometimes it seems that it's a person," she confessed, thinking about the shadowy figures from her nightmares and feeling her body react to the fear even now. "Then other times I'm not so sure." She stopped, giving her head a shake. "I don't know. Sometimes I wonder if I'm not Logan." She looked up at him and shrugged. "I just don't know."

Dr. McGhan lightly tapped the tips of his fingers together. "How do you feel about the name?"

"How do I feel about Logan? I'm not sure I know what you mean."

"The name Logan, does it solicit any particular response from you?"

"Well, yeah," she said sarcastically. "It makes me afraid to go to sleep."

"But what about now? Are you still afraid?"

She shifted again. "Not really. It just seems like a name now."

He tapped his fingertips together again, thinking. "It's interesting," he said after a moment, reaching up and grabbing at his glasses. "I think it might be a little more than just a name to you."

"What do you mean?"

"It's obvious you don't like talking about it. You don't even like saying it."

"I—I don't," she admitted.

"Why do you suppose that is?"

A rush of color filled her cheeks and she suddenly felt exposed and unprotected. That he could read her so easily made her feel foolish and had her feeling defensive.

"You're the doctor, you tell me," she snapped. It was apparent from his expression that the sarcasm had surprised him and she immediately felt bad. "Look, Dr. McGhan, I'm—I'm sorry," she added quickly, glancing down at her lap and curling her hands closed. "You're right. I don't like talking about this. It bothers me to think about those dreams, to think about Logan."

"Because it makes you feel frightened."

She nodded, thinking again of the icy fear of her nightmares and the warm comfort of Joe's arms. "Yes."

"It makes you feel helpless."

She paused for a moment. Now that she thought about it, he was right. "Does that seem important?"

"It could be," McGhan admitted. "The feelings you have for Logan—whomever or whatever Logan is or represents to you—are conflicted. It would make me think the name isn't one you feel possessive or particularly comfortable with."

"What would that mean?"

The doctor came forward in his chair. "To speculate a little, it would be my feeling that if Logan is a name, then it isn't yours."

Rain's eyes opened wide. "What makes you think that?"

"Like I said, I'm just speculating, but from what you say and your reaction, Logan represents something fearful to you. In other words, you don't get a warm fuzzy from it the way you did from…say…cooking." He lifted his hands in a small shrug. "And most people aren't afraid of their own names, especially in their subconscious."

Rain sat back again. "I never thought about it like that."

"Of course, that's not to say there couldn't be a dozen other explanations," he pointed out. "An abusive mate, a child, a relative." He pushed the chair back from the desk and stood up. "I'm just tossing around some thoughts." He walked around the desk, stopping in front of Rain and looking down at her. "I've treated a number of amnesia patients and there are no two cases alike, but they all seem to have one thing in common." He leaned back against the edge of the desk. "How they recover memories is never the same. There's a good chance you could experience a number of—" he lifted his hands, making quote signs with his fingers "—*recollections*—random images, feelings, impressions that pop into your head unexpectedly whether you're dreaming or awake. Some may turn out to be significant, some not, but I can tell you that to try to determine the significance of each one is impossible."

He reached down, slipping his hands over hers and helping her to her feet. "That's what we can do here— we'll talk about those random events, work with them, maybe try to make a little sense of them. What won't be helpful is for you to spend the rest of your time obsessing about things that might never make sense."

"Like Logan?"

Dr. McGhan nodded. "Maybe Logan is significant and maybe he's just a bogeyman left over from when you were a kid."

Bogeyman. She liked the perception of Logan as a figment of her imagination. She also like Dr. McGhan and left his office feeling more optimistic and hopeful than she had in days.

"All set?" Joe asked, quickly rising to his feet when she stepped into the doctor's waiting room.

"All set," she repeated. She swore he looked concerned, as though her well-being mattered to him, but she cautioned herself about losing perspective. She couldn't afford to do that with Logan and she couldn't with Joe Mountain, either.

"You wanted to see me?"

Joe looked up at the sound of Ryan's voice and frowned. "I wanted to see you twenty minutes ago."

Ryan shrugged, shifting his weight from one foot to the other. "Rain couldn't find the key for the postage machine. I was helping her look."

Joe rolled his eyes. Ryan had never hung around the office as much as he had in the last three weeks, but then Rain hadn't been working in the office until the last two weeks, either.

Almost a month. It seemed impossible to think that it had been over three weeks since Rain had walked out of the desert. Three weeks ago he would have thought they would have been much further along, would have thought they would have had something more to go on than they did, some concrete leads to follow.

Instead, he'd been slammed by one dead end after another. They had circulated photos of Rain to every agency, bureau, television station and newspaper this side of the Mississippi. They'd circulated the sketch of the man she'd described to the crime artist during their sessions together, but nothing had come of that either. Even the afternoon they had spent in the desert had failed to trigger anything. He'd driven her over every square inch of land in a fifty-mile radius from where

he'd found her, but try as she could, no memories were
forthcoming. They'd both gone home that night feeling
frustrated and thoroughly disappointed.

On a road to nowhere and frustrated by the brick
walls and blind alleys of unanswered questions, he'd
decided he'd waited long enough. He couldn't afford
to sit back and wait for something to come to him, he
had to get out there and make it happen.

He had stayed in the office late last night, poring
over missing persons reports for the umpteenth time,
examining and reexamining, looking for something he
might have missed, trying for a different angle, a new
light. But nothing had stood out, nothing he hadn't
seen and investigated a dozen times already. He'd gone
home feeling frustrated and thoroughly depressed.

The house had been dark when he'd gotten there.
Rain had no doubt turned in hours before. He'd for-
gone the dinner she had left out for him, restlessness
taking what little appetite he might have had. After
having checked on the stable and brushed down Sycamore, he'd gone up to bed feeling exhausted and
overwhelmed. Unfortunately, though, sleep just hadn't
been in the cards. After tossing and turning for the
better part of an hour, he'd flipped on the light and
reached for a sportsman's magazine on the nightstand.

A feature story on fly-fishing had seemed like just
the kind of slow-paced article that would put him right
to sleep, but something in the long-winded account had
him forgetting about his restlessness and had him sitting straight up in bed.

The article described a spot ideal for fly-fishing and
a company in Utah that manufactured a new kind of
lure. But it wasn't the advice about flies that had

caught his attention, but rather the name of the town itself. It all but leapt off the page at him.

Logan.

He'd gotten up and torn the house apart looking for a map, eventually finding one to confirm what he'd read. It had taken a little searching, but sure enough, there it had been in the northernmost part of the state, right off Highway 91—Logan, Utah, population 32,762.

"Going somewhere?" Ryan asked, pointing at the road map spread out on the desk.

"Didn't you say you had a buddy who was a deputy sheriff somewhere in Utah?" Joe asked, ignoring the questions as he turned back to the map.

"Kane County," Ryan said, pointing to a shaded area on the map. "Just the other side of the border."

"That's what I thought. How good a buddy is he?"

"He's not a buddy exactly," Ryan explained, giving him a skeptical look. "Just some guy who dated my sister for a while."

Joe looked up from the map. "I hope they parted in good company."

Ryan's gaze narrowed and he gave Joe a suspicious look. "Why?"

Reaching for the telephone, Joe handed the receiver to Ryan. "Because you're going to call your old buddy and ask him for a favor."

"What?" Ryan looked down at the telephone in his hand as though he'd never seen one before. "What kind of favor?"

"Call him up, ask him if he's got any connection in Cache County. There's something I want to check out in that area."

"Cache County! That's way the hell north of Kane."

"So I want you to call your friend and find out if he knows anyone up there." Joe reached for his hat as he headed for the door. "If not, ask him if he could make a few phone calls and find out who would be the best person to talk to. I want information on any missing persons, runaways, abductions—anything like that."

"But we've got all that information from the Justice Department's database," Ryan pointed out.

"We got the official stuff. What I want is all the stuff that doesn't get reported. The rumors, the assaults, the domestic calls nobody bothers to report on."

"Okay, but what if he doesn't know anyone?"

Joe stopped when he reached the door and turned around. "Then I'm just going to do some poking around on my own."

"How long you gonna be gone?"

"Don't know," he said, snapping his fingers. "And don't mention anything to Rain about where I'm going."

Ryan frowned. "Why not?"

"I just don't—"

"Oh, wait," Ryan interrupted, slapping his forehead. "Wait a minute. Cache County. Logan! I get it now. You're going up to Logan."

Joe's eyes opened wide. "You've heard of the place?"

"Only because I broke down there once—that piece of garbage pickup I used to have." Ryan looked up at him, the wheels beginning to turn. "Yeah, Logan. Is that what she could be talking about? Logan, Utah?"

"Don't know, but it's worth a trip to find out."

"Damn straight," Ryan said, his enthusiasm building as he reached for the phone. "I'll get on the horn to Jim in Wheeler and see if he's got any connections up there."

"Good, and I meant it when I said not to say anything to Rain," Joe reiterated, stopping Ryan before he could dial the number. "This could turn out to be a wild-goose chase. No point letting her get her hopes up—not yet, anyway. Let me see if I come up with something first."

Ryan nodded, his face serious. "Understood. She's had enough disappointments as it is."

Joe turned for the door. Ryan did understand. Driving up to Utah was a long shot, but they both had been in law enforcement long enough to know that cases had been solved on a lot less. While nothing Rain had said indicated the Logan from her nightmares was a place and not a person, it really didn't matter. When you had nothing to go on, you start grabbing at straws.

"You're leaving?"

Joe stopped at the sound of Rain's voice, fumbling the car keys in his hand. "Uh, yeah."

"Going to be gone long?"

He quickly glanced away. She had every right to ask. There would be telephone calls and people wanting to talk to him, but his conscience had him feeling guilty.

"Uh, yeah," he stammered, shooting her a guilty glance.

"Okay," she said with a smile, giving him a little wave.

"Ryan will drive you out to the house when you're ready to go," he added quickly, turning back for the door.

"Oh."

He didn't have to see her face to know that her smile had faded. He could hear it in her voice.

"You won't be coming back to the office at all?"

He stopped and looked up, hoping he didn't look as awkward and uncomfortable as he felt. "Probably not."

"Is there something you'd like me to do then?" she asked. Her smile faltered despite her efforts to stop it. "At the house? Maybe with Sycamore?"

He felt small. "Not necessary. Charlie will take care of everything. If you need anything though, give him a shout."

"I will," she said in a quiet voice. "Maybe I could leave something out for your dinner?"

"Don't bother," he insisted. She had such a wounded expression it only made him feel worse. He was only trying to protect her, only trying keep her from getting hurt—again—and it was all he could do to stop himself from blurting out everything. "I'll pick up something while I'm out. But thanks anyway."

He turned and left quickly, rushing out the door and across the parking lot before she had a chance to say anything else. Frankly, he wasn't sure how much more he could have taken. Her feelings had been hurt. He hadn't liked doing that, but it wasn't the first time in the last week that he'd hurt her. The week had been hell.

He'd been determined to make himself back away from her, determined to keep himself on track, but he was finding the only way he could do that was to simply stay away. He'd found one excuse after another to keep from going home at night. He'd stayed at the office late, gone on late patrols—anything and everything he could think of that would get him back to the house long after she'd gone up to bed.

It had been such an abrupt change, such a shift from the way it had been the first few days she'd been with him. Then they'd been together practically every waking hour, eating meals together and helping each other out at the office and around the house. The change had not gone unnoticed, causing a strain between them and the tension in the last few days had become almost unbearable.

He took full responsibility for everything. If a problem had developed between them, it was by his design. She'd done nothing wrong, nothing more than be a cheerful, friendly house mate with a sunny disposition and optimistic outlook. He'd been the one to change, the one looking for excuses to stay away.

While she'd had no major breakthrough as far as recovered memories, her sessions with Dr. McGhan seemed to be helping. She seemed stronger, more content and less anxious. She worked hard while at the office, having expanded her job to not only filing and answering the telephone, but having discovered herself to be quite an accomplished typist, she now worked on the computer, typing all their reports and correspondence. Ryan was enraptured by the woman, not to mention Walt and Sal at the diner.

Joe climbed into his Jeep and slipped the key into the ignition. But he knew the truth. He knew her life was far from perfect. He saw through her upbeat manner and optimistic smile. He heard her at night when she thought he was asleep, he heard her pacing the floor after the nightmares had awakened her. Even now he could hear her quiet sobs in his head, tears in the darkness that had begun to haunt him, too.

She was remarkable and to say she was making the most of an impossible situation would be an understatement. But the truth of the matter was she wanted her life back, she deserved it back and he'd been unable to give it to her. He'd never felt so helpless or so useless in his life.

Shifting the Jeep into gear, he pulled out of the parking lot, swearing under his breath. So who was he really going to Utah for—for her, or himself? Did he honestly think he was going to find something or was he looking for justification, looking for another excuse to stay out of the house and away from her?

He'd tried to tell himself that he needed his space, that the woman had invaded his life and he was feeling hemmed in and trapped, but that was just an excuse. The brutal truth was he liked having her in his house, cooking his meals and accompanying him to work. He liked having someone to talk to, someone to worry about him, someone to comfort. He liked that she'd taken an interest in his horses, in his friends and in his life.

He pulled onto the highway, pushing the accelerator to the floor. That was just it, that was the problem, that was why he had to stay away—he liked it too much.

"What's this?"

"Your paycheck."

Rain glanced down at the envelope in her hand and felt her heart do a trip in her chest. "My paycheck?"

Joe nodded, stepping away from her desk. "I had the county registrar draft it in cash, even though she was able to get a temporary Social Security number issued for you."

Rain gingerly opened the envelope, looking at the bills inside. "You mean all this? It's mine?"

"Sure," Ryan said as he walked to the water cooler and poured himself a drink. "What did you think? We were going to charge you for the pleasure of working you long hours?"

Rain looked up, turning to Joe. "But I can't take this."

Joe stopped. "What do you mean you can't take it?"

"It's…it's too much. You've already done too much."

"That's ridiculous," he scoffed. "You earned it. It's your money. Just take it."

She glanced down at the envelope again. It had never occurred to her she'd be paid for the job she was doing. She'd just been grateful to have something to do, that she had some way of paying Joe back for having taken her in, for having clothed and fed her. Although lately, she'd begun to think that maybe the best way she could thank him for all his kindness would be to get out of his life.

The past few weeks had been difficult. Joe was barely speaking to her and when he did, he seemed short and surly. She couldn't deny that his impatience hadn't hurt, but she really couldn't blame him.

When he'd invited her to stay at the ranch, they both had understood that it was to be a temporary arrangement. After all, she had a life out there somewhere and through therapy and healing, one day she would have it back. She just hadn't realized it would take so long. She also hadn't realized how much she would come to love Joe Mountain's ranch and the life she had there.

But week after week had passed and she was no

closer now to knowing who she was or what had happened to her than she'd been on that first morning she'd awakened in the hospital. Her world might have started a short month ago, but his hadn't and it was obvious from the way he'd been acting the last couple of weeks that he was losing patience with her lack of progress.

He had an entire life filled with a ranch and a career, and she wasn't a part of it. She was a visitor to his world—a guest who had outstayed her welcome.

"Thank you," she murmured, slipping the money into the pocket of one of Karen Mountain's hand-me-down sweaters.

"I'll take you over to the bank later if you'd like," he said, the kindness of the offer dampened by the impatient tone of his voice. "Not good to carry around that much cash. You could open up an account if you like."

"Uh, thanks, but that's not necessary," she said. "No need for you to bother. I can take care of that myself."

"Whatever," he said with a shrug. "It's your money."

The look of surprise on his face when she'd refused his offer had been subtle, but it had been there and she couldn't help feeling just a little pleased. Maybe she had been too dependent on him and maybe it was time she started getting out and doing a few things on her own.

She had learned a lot about Joe Mountain and his world since she'd gone to live in his house, but she had also learned a lot about herself. Not only had she discovered she knew how to cook, she'd also learned she was computer literate, well versed in classic literature and music and had a distinct talent for crossword puzzles. Maybe now it was time to see if she had an independent streak, as well.

"Open for business?"

Rain turned to the door just as an attractive woman stepped into the office.

"We're always open for Superior Court Judges," Joe said, quickly rounding the desk. "Especially those who have been carrying on the county's business at a different venue."

"How's the trial going, Judge?" Ryan asked with a teasing smile. "Juries up in Carson City a little friendlier than they are around here?"

"Juries are juries," she said, giving Ryan a wave. She turned to Joe, giving him a hug. "I'm just glad to be home."

"Glad to have you back, Your Honor," Joe said, gazing down at her. "Stopping by to see if we've arrested anyone lately?"

There was no denying the affection in his eyes when he looked at the woman and Rain felt sick to her stomach. She wished she could just shrivel up and disappear.

The woman was striking in a cream-colored silk suit that draped her tall, slender frame with perfection. The rich leather briefcase and handbag she carried looked classy and professional, making Rain feel all the more dowdy in her borrowed clothes.

"Actually, Sheriff, I didn't come to see you."

"No? I'm wounded."

"Good thing you're not under oath," she said dryly, giving him a playful push aside. "Or I'm afraid a charge of perjury might be in order. Actually I came by to meet your friend.'' She turned and started toward the desk. ''I want to meet Rain.''

For a moment Rain thought she hadn't heard right. ''Me?''

''Absolutely,'' the woman said, extending a hand across the desk. ''Hello, Rain, I'm Marcy Martinez.''

''Actually, she is the Honorable Marcy Martinez,'' Joe corrected as Rain gingerly took the Judge's hand. ''Marcy's married to Cruz.''

''You're...'' Rain's voice cracked and faded and she had to clear her throat before she could speak again. ''You're married to Dr. Martinez?''

Marcy nodded. ''And I have to apologize for not coming by earlier. I was there at the hospital the night Joe brought you in, but I've been out of town since then. But I'm back now, and I wanted to come by and maybe see if we could get together for lunch sometime.''

''Lunch?''

''Yeah, what do you say?''

Rain felt a little overwhelmed right now. After all, the woman was beautiful and seeing her in Joe Mountain's arms had been a little unnerving. But there was something about Marcy Martinez that was so genuine, so engaging, it was hard to resist. Besides, aside from Carrie in the hospital and Sal at the diner, there were no women in her life. Marcy Martinez was extending a hand of friendship and Rain found herself wanting very much to accept.

''I—I'd love to,'' she stammered.

''I'd make her pay, Judge,'' Ryan added. ''She just got her first paycheck.''

Marcy's eyes opened wide. ''Really?''

Rain's hand went to the envelope of money in her sweater pocket. "I did."

Marcy thought for a moment, then leaned close. "You know, I was thinking of heading up to Reno. They're having a big sale at the mall there. Feel like playing hooky?"

Chapter 9

"**W**hy Rain?"

"I'm not sure," Rain admitted. "Carrie said Joe had called me that when he'd brought me into the hospital. It just stuck."

"I guess that makes sense," Marcy said. "And it's better than Jane Doe."

Jane Doe. Rain turned the name over in her brain. It felt cold and unfamiliar. She'd never felt that way about the name Joe had given to her. Despite the wet element it described, as a name it had felt warm, felt right to her. She didn't know what name she'd answered to before, but in the weeks she'd lived in Mesa Ridge, she'd become Rain.

"Much better," she agreed.

Marcy's expression turned thoughtful. "I can only imagine how difficult it's been for you. I don't know what I'd do if I woke up and...and there was nothing there."

Rain thought back to that awful moment in the desert when there had just been the rain and the cold and the fear. "It was terrifying at first," she admitted. "Actually, there are times when it's terrifying even now. But everyone has been so kind. Your husband is a wonderful doctor, by the way, and I'm happy with my sessions with Dr. McGhan."

Marcy smiled. "So you're feeling hopeful then?"

"Hopeful," she conceded. "But I can't let myself think about it too much. I get so...so discouraged sometimes, too. I know the doctors tell me not to try to force it, but it's so *frustrating*. I mean, isn't there someone out there wondering about me? Doesn't someone want to know where I am or what happened to me? Did I have no one in my life? Isn't there someone worried about me?" She stopped and shook her head. "Sometimes I just want to—" her hands balled into fists "—sometimes I just want to scream."

Marcy reached across the table, giving her arm a pat. "This really is difficult for you, isn't it? More difficult than you let on."

Rain put her head down, feeling the sting of tears burn her eyes. "Everyone has been so wonderful to me. I feel so awkward...so ungrateful...I don't mean to complain...."

"Wanting your life back isn't complaining," Marcy assured her, giving her arm squeeze. "I think if things seem awkward at times, it's only because people don't know what to say. It's so sad, your whole life has just been taken away."

"Erased, like chalk off a blackboard," Rain said. She sat up suddenly. She was almost becoming accustomed to those unexpected rushes of familiarity—almost.

"What is it?"

She thought for a moment, then looked at Marcy. "Nothing. It's nothing. Just every once in a while I get this feeling, like I almost remember, but—" she gave her head a shake "—it goes away. Dr. McGhan says it's normal." She shook her head again. "I think it feels anything but normal."

Marcy reached for her coffee cup, taking a sip. "Well, I think it's wonderful how you're keeping yourself busy, working at the sheriff's office. I'm impressed."

"I'm grateful to have something to do, something to take my mind off myself. I'd go crazy if I didn't have somewhere to go every morning." She shifted in the seat. "Besides, it's the least I can do. The sheriff has been very generous, giving me a place to stay and all." She felt her throat tighten up. He had been kind and she hated to think how she'd overstayed her welcome. "But we've talked enough about me. You're a judge. I find that so interesting."

"I'm a superior court judge," Marcy corrected playfully, popping a piece of cheesecake into her mouth. "In the judge business, that's important. You get to boss everyone around and tell people what to do and they pay you for it. Is that great or what?"

Rain laughed, letting her fork drop to her place and leaning back in her chair. She'd had the most remarkable day. She couldn't remember if she'd ever had a girlfriend before, if she'd ever spent a day shopping and having lunch and talking and sharing the biggest, richest, most fattening piece of cheesecake with a girlfriend before, but she had today. Marcy Fitzgerald Martinez was wonderful and their day of shopping had been more than just an outing, more than two friends getting together; it had been a bonding.

"Well, if I don't stop eating," she groaned, pushing herself back from the table, "I'm not going to be able to get into those new clothes I just bought."

"I swear, I don't know where you put it," Marcy commented, surveying the empty plates in front of Rain. "You eat like a truck driver but you're just a little bit of a thing." She reached for her coffee cup. "I think I hate you."

"I do have a healthy appetite."

Marcy turned and surveyed the stack of packages piled up on the booth beside them. "All in all, I'd say you did all right today, considering this is your first time out."

Rain thought of all the beautiful clothes she'd bought and smiled. She couldn't wait to try them on again, and for Joe to see her in something other than his ex-wife's wardrobe.

"First time. Does that mean we can to do this again?"

"Sure," Marcy said with a grin. "How about next payday?" They both laughed again. "But seriously," Marcy added as their laughter faded. "I think you really made the most of those sales. At least you've got enough things there to get you out of Karen Mountain's hand-me-downs."

Rain glanced down at the pink sweater, its harsh color all the more garish in the bright lights of the restaurant. "They are pretty awful, aren't they?" She looked back up at Marcy. "Did you know her?"

"Karen?" Marcy shook her head. "No. Actually Annie and I only moved to Mesa Ridge two years ago—when Cruz and I got married. Karen was long gone before that. Cruz had met her, though.''

"Really?'' Rain did her best to make her voice sound casual. ''Did he ever say what she was like?''

"Not really. He just said she never seemed like a very happy person.''

"She lived on that beautiful ranch, had that terrific house,'' Rain mused. She glanced up at Marcy and shrugged. ''You'd think she would have been on top of the world.''

"You'd think, but ranch life in an place like Mesa Ridge isn't for everyone,'' Marcy pointed out. ''It probably wasn't her cup of tea. And besides, from what Cruz has told me about their breakup, I'd say maybe things worked out for the best.'' She leaned close, her voice lowering. ''I don't even know the woman but judging from what I've seen of her wardrobe, I'd say all her taste was in her mouth anyway.''

Rain laughed, but she was too distracted to find any true humor. Her mind was racing with so many questions, so many things she wanted to know. Still, she understood there was always a risk in asking questions, that she ran the risk of getting an answer she didn't like. But Marcy had peaked her curiosity talking about Karen Mountain and she couldn't help but be curious about the woman who Joe had made his wife, the woman he never mentioned, never spoke about.

"Were they married long, do you know?''

"Karen and Joe?'' Marcy thought for a moment. ''I don't think so, a year or so. From what I understand, things fell apart pretty fast once Karen lost the baby.''

Rain felt the hair tingle on the back of her neck and the breath seemed to stall in her lungs. ''There…there was a baby?''

Marcy nodded. "Karen had gone into premature labor. By the time she got to the hospital, there were other complications and she'd miscarried." Marcy sipped at her coffee. "Apparently they were together for only a few months after that."

"How awful," Rain sighed. No wonder he didn't want to talk about her; how painful the memories must be.

"I don't think it was a very amicable divorce, either," Marcy continued. "I really don't know any of the specifics, but from what Cruz has said, Joe took it pretty hard."

"I can imagine," Rain murmured. "To lose your child and then your wife. That would be hard for anyone."

"And Joe keeps things pretty close to the chest," Marcy added. "But then, I'm sure I don't have to tell you that. He doesn't let many people get close."

Rain nodded, suddenly finding it a little difficult to swallow. He'd made it pretty clear he didn't want her too close, either.

"It was really wonderful of him to take me in, give me a place to stay, a job," she said, the words feeling tight in her throat. "I'm not sure what I would have done if…" She grabbed the napkin from her lap and tossed it on to the table. "Well, I'm really grateful to him for all he's done but I think it's time I start looking for a place of my own."

Marcy's eyes widened. "You don't like it out there on the ranch?"

"Oh, I love it," Rain contended.

"Then why leave? It's a big house. Joe just rattles around in that place by himself."

Rain glanced down, reaching for a spoon on the table and absently tapping it against the crumpled napkin. "It's just...I have no idea how long...well, if I'll ever..." She looked up and gave her head a small shake. "I could go on like this for a long time, not knowing what happened to me, not knowing where I belong, where I live, who I am. I can't expect to stay with Joe—I mean, Sheriff Mountain—indefinitely. He's been wonderful, but he's got a life of his own and I feel a little like I'm in the way. I don't want to overstay my welcome and I can't keep leaning on him, depending on him forever."

Marcy regarded her for a long moment—so long, in fact, that Rain began to feel uncomfortable under her scrutiny.

"You want my honest opinion?"

"Of—of course," Rain said, wondering now if she did.

"I think you're the best thing that happened to Joe Mountain in years."

The spoon slipped from her fingers, landing with the clank against the wood tabletop. "What?"

"I mean it," she insisted. "Joe Mountain needs to get involved in life again. He's a wonderful man, but he's resisted any involvements for as long as I've known him. All he does is work and take care of those horses of his—and occasionally go fishing with my husband. There's more to life than that."

"But that is his life," Rain pointed out. "The life he wants."

Marcy shook her head and smiled. "Tell me I'm being a typical woman thinking I know what's good for every man I meet, but—" her smile faded as she leaned forward in the booth "—I think he needs more than that. I'm not saying I think you should stay there forever, but I seriously doubt you're in the way out there. You're good for him. You give him something other than Mesa County and those horses to think about.''

Rain wondered if Nevada was susceptible to earthquakes because she was certain the ground beneath her had trembled. She didn't know what to say, was barely able to think. As much as she wanted to believe what Marcy said was true, it seemed impossible given the cold, distant way Joe had been acting lately.

''Do you know what happened to her?'' Rain asked after a moment, changing the subject. Talking about her relationship with Joe was too awkward, too uncomfortable, especially when she wasn't entirely sure there was much of a relationship to talk about. ''His wife I mean?''

''No,'' Marcy said, shaking her head. ''Nothing more than she left Mesa Ridge lock, stock and barrel—except for those awful clothes.''

''Well, I won't miss them,'' Rain admitted, picking up one of the bags from beside her and peeking inside.

''I know I didn't,'' Marcy said, spearing the last morsel of cheesecake from the plate.

''Wait a minute, wait a minute,'' Rain said, stopping as she reached for another of bag, and turned to Marcy. ''You wore Karen Mountain's clothes?''

Marcy laughed as she reached for the check. ''It's a long story and I'll tell you all about it sometime, but not now.'' Reaching into her purse, she pulled out several bills, leaving them on the small tray for the waiter. ''Now, we've got more shopping to do.'' Gathering up her bags, she slid out of the booth. ''But just make sure if Joe starts talking about taking you up to 'the boonies,' that you pack your own things. Otherwise you'll be stuck with more of Karen's frumpy frocks.''

"The boonies?"

"I told you, it's long story," Marcy said again, her smile turning into a grin. "A very long story."

He heard the car in the drive, heard footsteps on the porch and the sound of the back door opening. She was back.

Letting out a long, slow breath, he leaned his head back against the chair and turned to gaze out the window. The moon had risen high in the sky, drenching everything in a creamy glow and making the night seem all the more surreal.

He didn't need to check his watch. He already knew it was late. He'd been sitting alone in the dark since he'd gotten home, sitting and waiting. He'd had too much to drink, too much of the white man's "fire water" and he was feeling very Navajo right now. The alcohol surged through his system, making his mind think crazy and his blood burn hot.

She'd been gone the entire day, having left with Marcy this morning to go shopping. Of course he had no reason to worry. She was with Marcy, the two of them were just fine. They were having a wonderful time and had even decided to take in a movie and dinner before starting back for Mesa Ridge. However, he hadn't found that out because Rain hadn't bothered to call and tell him. He'd talked with Cruz. Marcy had telephoned him earlier to check in and to keep him posted of her whereabouts so that he wouldn't be worried.

Rain hadn't bothered to let him know. Apparently

she didn't care if he worried—or perhaps, she just didn't care.

He heard her in the kitchen, her shoes stepping lightly along the tile. He had no right to be angry, no right to be upset. After all, to her he was merely the sheriff into whose county she'd wandered, the official who had befriended her, the person whose job it was to find out who she was and what had happened to her out there in the desert—a job he hadn't had much success in lately.

His trip to Logan, Utah, last week had been a bust. None of its residents were missing, none had any relatives missing, none knew of *anyone* missing and none of them recognized the photos of Rain he'd taken with him. And yet he had stayed on—longer than he needed to, longer than he should have. He'd poked and prodded, chasing down one far-fetched theory after another.

He'd never felt so worthless, so completely ineffective as he had driving back to Mesa Ridge with nothing. He was barely able to face her. She'd looked to him for help, looked to him to find the answers she needed and he'd let her down. He had nothing to offer, no reason to give or explanation to make for what had happened. He was beginning to believe she really was like the rain, borne of the clouds and whose life had begun that dark, stormy night on the desert.

So she didn't owe him anything, least of all a call to let him know she was all right so he wouldn't worry. Besides that, he was the one who'd been telling himself all week that he needed space, needed time away from her.

So why was he sitting there in the dark feeling betrayed? Depressed and guilty over his inability to help her, he'd looked for excuses not to go home. How many times had he stayed away without bothering to tell her where he was going or when he'd be back? What made him think he deserved the kind of courtesy he'd failed to show her?

He took another swig of beer, draining the can and crushing it flat. Maybe he hadn't been very nice to her lately, maybe he had pulled away, stayed out late and hadn't bothered to tell her where he was or when he'd be back. Maybe he had no right to expect her to think about his feelings when he hadn't bothered to think about hers. Maybe...

He tossed the can down. It dropped soundlessly to the carpet, disappearing in the darkness. Damn it, why hadn't she called him? Didn't she think he might worry? Didn't she think he had a right to know she was all right? She was Rain, *his* Rain. He'd found her, he'd taken care of her, he was the one sitting in the dark worrying about her. Didn't that count for something?

The footsteps grew louder. She had left the kitchen and was heading for the stairs. She would pass the living room, pass right by him, but it was so dark she would never see him. All he had to do was sit there and not move, sit there and let her pass, let her find her way up to her room. She'd never have to know he'd waited up for her, never have to know how much he'd had to drink and how crazy he was thinking.

"You're back."

Even as he saw her jump violently and skitter to a stop, he couldn't believe those words had actually come out of his mouth.

"J-Joe?" she gasped, several of her packages slipping to the floor. "Is that you?"

"You were expecting someone else?"

The room tilted dangerously when he stood, and his reached for the arms of the chair to steady himself.

"I wasn't expecting anyone," she admitted. As she bent to retrieve her packages, two more slipped from her grasp. "You gave me quite a start."

"Here, let me help you with those," he said gallantly as he started across the dark room. Unfortunately, his boot found the crushed beer can at that moment, sending him hurling toward her.

"Joe!" she shrieked as he crashed into her, sending the rest of her packages spilling to the floor.

"Have you been..." Despite the dim lighting, he could see her eyes grow wide. "Joe, you've been drinking."

The fact that it was so obvious made him defensive. "A—a few beers." The disappointment in her eyes was almost more than he could take. She had no right to make him feel guilty. He was the one who'd been left without a call. He was the one who'd been left to worry. "Last time I checked, that wasn't against the law."

"No, of course not," she said, slowly bending down to reach for her packages. "I—I didn't mean to disturb you."

He lunged for the packages, too, snatching them up before she had a chance. "That must have been some shopping trip you went on."

"I was able to get a few things," she said, reaching for the bags.

"I've got them," he insisted, motioning with his chin to the stairway. "I'll take them up."

"No, no," she said, shaking her head and reaching for them again. "I don't want to bother you. I can do—"

"I've got them," he stated flatly, cutting her off.

She hesitated for a moment before turning for the steps and something surged angry and hot through his system. Was she afraid of him? Was she afraid to be alone in the house with a drunken savage?

What other reason did you think I'd let you touch me? Because I loved you? How could I love you? You're an...an Indian.

Karen's words burned in his brain, bringing back the memories, bringing back the shame.

"I hope I didn't disturb you, coming in so late," she said as she climbed the stairs ahead of him. "It must be close to nine."

"It's nine-thirty," he corrected.

"Is it really?" She stopped at the door to her bedroom. "I had no idea." She pushed the door open and flipped on the light. "We were just having such a great time we decided to—"

"Have some dinner and take in a movie, I know," he said, hearing the anger in his voice. Stepping into the room behind her, he deposited the packages on the bed. "I talked to Cruz. I was ready to put out an APB on you two."

"I'm sorry. I probably should have called—"

"That would have been nice," he said, interrupting her again.

She stopped as she reached for one of the bags, slowly turning to him. "Then again, I guess I just didn't figure we were checking in with one another."

There was challenge in her eyes, confrontation. He'd never seen her like that before. She'd fired a shot that had hit the very center of the target. After all, he hadn't bothered to keep her posted on his comings or goings.

But instead of feeling defensive and touchy, he was

feeling something different—something very different. Maybe it was the alcohol in his system, maybe it was the emotion he saw in her eyes or maybe it was just the fact that he was there with her in her bedroom, but whatever the cause, fire began to surge through his system.

"I guess I thought..."

"What did you think, Joe?" she asked when his words drifted off. "Tell me, I want to know."

Heat surged to his brain causing his eyes to blur and his cheeks to feel flush. The challenge was still there in her eyes but he could see something else, as well. Passion. It was brash, it was reckless and it was real.

"I think," he murmured in a voice barely above a whisper. Reaching out, he caught her by the arms, dragging her to him. "I think I want you."

Her lips tasted sweet, far sweeter than he'd imagined, far sweeter than he'd ever known. It was as if he couldn't get enough of their flavor, couldn't get enough of her. He crushed his mouth tight to hers, her soft lips feeling warm and velvety against his. He wasn't sure what had happened to him. Suddenly he was so hungry for her, so desperate for her, craving her like an addict craving his particular drug of choice.

Suddenly he had become one with nature, one with the earth and the elements—sunlight, moonlight, stars, clouds, Rain, Rain, Rain.

She melted against him, her soft, warm body melding against his as though it were made to be there. The need became everything—life, breath and sustenance. He wasn't Joe, wasn't the law, wasn't Navajo. With her in his arms he was not merely a man, he became every man, and she was the only woman he wanted.

"Joe," she groaned against his lips. Her voice was

raw, its husky tone communicating so much more than the word she'd uttered, telling him of longing and desire, of hunger and need.

And for Joe, it was like a glass of ice water in the face. Reality rumbled through his system like a shock wave, jolting him like a tremor ripping through the earth's crust leaving him wide-awake and cold stone sober.

What was he doing? What was he thinking? Was he thinking at all? He had no right kissing her, no right to even touch her and he had no right at all in wanting her.

The woman trusted him, she needed him, but not to take advantage of her, not to hit on her when she was her most vulnerable—and she certainly didn't need him to kiss her. She needed him to be the sheriff, to be the man who would help her solve the mystery of her past. She was his responsibility. This was his county, his town and it was his duty to help her in any way that he could.

Only in the last few weeks he seemed to have forgotten about that. Somehow, someway she'd stopped being just an unsolved case. She had become a person to him, a *real* person—the only person he thought about any more and a woman he found he wanted very much.

"I—I can't do this," he said, grabbing her by the arms and abruptly setting her away from him.

"Joe," she whispered in protest, giving her head a shake. "I don't...I don't understand."

The look of hurt and disappointment in her eyes was almost more than he could take. It was all he could do to stop himself from pulling her back into his arms and ravishing her mouth with his again.

"I'm sorry," he said, the words sounding as painful as they felt saying them. "This isn't right."

It was a lie. Nothing in his life had ever felt so right, but he couldn't think about that. He turned for the door. He had to get out of there, had to get away from her before he lost what fragile hold on caution and common sense, reality and duty he had left.

At the door, he stopped, but dared not turn around.

"I'm really sorry," he said again before rushing out of the bedroom, closing the door behind him.

Chapter 10

It wasn't right. That was what he'd said and it was what she had to believe. It wasn't right that she was still living in his house, wasn't right that he'd kissed her and it wasn't right that she wanted him. It simply wasn't right.

Rain squeezed her eyes tight, blocking out the faint, predawn light and feeling the burn of tears. The sun hadn't yet peeked over the horizon, but the pale, milky glow of the sky foreshadowed its arrival. Soon light would be pouring in through the sash windows and it would be time to start another day again.

But she wasn't ready for the harsh light of day just yet. She wanted the darkness to swallow her up and take all the hurt away.

The night had been endless. She'd been exhausted when she'd returned home after her shopping adventure with Marcy and yet she'd barely slept a wink all night. She'd been restless and uncomfortable, unable to settle down. All she'd done was toss and turn and think about Joe—the feel of him, the taste of him and the desire that had arced between them.

But had it been desire? She couldn't tell any longer. She didn't know what was real and what wasn't—what was right and what was wrong. She had thought they were becoming friends, had thought he'd come to care about her on more than just a professional level, but it was obvious now that she'd been wrong about that. In the last several weeks he'd barely talked to her, had barely wanted to spend any time with her at all. He'd even had Ryan drive her to her last appointment with Dr. McGhan so he didn't have to be bothered. That was hardly the way friends treated one another.

"Okay, so we're not friends," she said aloud, opening her eyes and staring up at the fading shadows along the ceiling.

She couldn't deny that the realization hurt, because it had—a lot—but she was doing her best to accept it. She'd been trying to stay out of his way, trying not to be a freeloader and just live off of his good graces. She did what she could to help around the house— cooking and cleaning—not that it mattered, though. He barely ate anything she cooked any longer and he wasn't around enough to notice how clean the place was.

Which was why it had surprised her to come back to find him so angry. She would have thought he would have liked it that she'd been out, that he would have liked to have had the house to himself for most of the evening. But instead he'd been short and curt with her, in every way acting annoyed that she'd been out so late.

"We're not friends," she said again, the light through the windows glowing brighter.

But if they weren't friends, what were they?

She thought about the kiss, about the way he had grabbed her, the way he had held her. There had been nothing hesitant or shy in his actions, nothing ambiguous or unclear in their intent. They had been decisive and determined. And there had been nothing chaste or reserved about the kiss, either. It had been deliberate and intentional and wildly passionate.

"But it wasn't right," she whispered, closing her eyes again.

And it wasn't right. It didn't matter that it had felt right; it didn't matter that she wanted it to be right. She had lost her objectivity where Joe Mountain was concerned weeks ago.

She didn't know what was right and what was wrong any longer. She couldn't rely on her feelings because it was painfully clear that where he was concerned, her feelings had steered her wrong. And since she had no memories, no experiences, nothing from the past to fall back on, she had to trust that what he said was the truth. Whatever it was that had happened between them last night hadn't been right.

She closed her eyes again, feeling tears spilling out and onto the pillow. It was stupid to cry, stupid to think that he could come to care for her. She had nothing to offer—no name and no past—and who knew what the future would hold? No man in his right mind would want to get involved with a woman who could at any moment turn out to be another person entirely. She was Rain now, but once her memories came back, she would be someone else, anything else—a doctor, a lawyer, a nun, a con artist or even a criminal.

She groaned, swiping at the tears, and turned onto her side. It seemed like such an impossible situation. She liked her life in Mesa Ridge, liked being Rain; but at the same time she wanted desperately to recover her past, wanted to know who she'd been and what she'd done with her life. But what if the answers weren't what she wanted? What if she didn't like the person she'd been? If Joe Mountain didn't like her now, would he like her then?

She jumped at the sound of the back door, surprised when she turned to see Joe step inside.

"Oh, you're back," she said, quickly turning back to the soup she had cooking on the stove. She felt self-conscious in her bare feet and wearing only the over-size nightshirt she'd bought on her shopping spree yesterday. "I'd thought you were planning to spend the night up in Reno?"

"Things broke up early," he mumbled, walking to the refrigerator and pulling out a bottle of beer.

Rain kept her eyes glued to the soup bubbling in the saucepan, but every sense she had made her aware of his every move. After an exhausting night with little sleep, the day had been long and tiring. Joe had given her a ride to work this morning, dropping her off at the office before leaving.

He'd said little during their drive into town, not that she'd expected more. Still, it would have been nice and maybe taken a little of the sting out of his rejection. After all, he *had* kissed her. The least he could have done was acknowledge that. Maybe it hadn't meant much to him but did that give him the right to just ignore it, to pretend it never happened?

In her peripheral vision, she could see him twist off

the cap from the beer bottle and take a long drink and a disturbing thought crept into her head, something she hadn't thought about until now. Joe had been drinking last night, and from his slurred speech and clumsy movements he'd been drinking quite a bit. Was it possible he didn't remember the kiss? Could it be that all the passion and all the desire she'd thought she'd sensed last night were simply a result of too much alcohol?

She gave her head a shake. What did it matter? It was over, it was a mistake and by his own words, it wasn't right. Maybe she would be better off if she tried to forget it, too.

"I'm just fixing a little soup, you're welcome to have some if you'd like."

He took another drink, a long one this time. "Yeah, that would be great."

The spoon in her hand dropped, landing with a clank against the side of the saucepan. "You will?"

He nodded. "If it's not too much trouble."

"N-no, of course not," she stammered, reaching for the handle of the spoon.

How many times in the last few weeks had she asked him to share a meal with her and how many times had he refused? She'd asked fully expecting him to refuse this time, too, but he'd managed to surprise her again. She almost wished now she hadn't asked. She felt so uncomfortable around him, so ill at ease she almost preferred to be alone.

She'd actually been relieved when he'd told her about his meeting this morning. Things had become so tense and uncomfortable, she actually looked forward to an evening to herself. After her long conversation with Marcy this morning, she'd had a lot to think about, a lot of plans to make.

"Need any help with anything?" he asked.

"Not much to do," she confessed with a shrug. "You could get those wheat crackers in the pantry if you'd like. I thought I'd slice some cheese."

"Oh, yeah, cheese and crackers sound good with the soup," he said, setting down his beer and disappearing into the pantry. "I hope this isn't too much bother."

"No bother at all," she said as he reappeared from the pantry with the box of crackers in his hand. He was being almost friendly, which only made what she had to tell him all that much harder. "Like I said, it's just soup and crackers and there's plenty." She hesitated for only a moment, dropping her gaze to the soup again. "Besides we need to talk."

From the corner of her eye she saw him stop abruptly.

"Talk?"

She nodded.

He set the cracker box down on the table. "Sure, what's up?"

"Well, let's get the soup poured," she said, her courage deserting her as she pulled two bowls down from the cupboard and reached for the ladle. "Might as well, while it's hot."

The meal was casual, with the two of them sitting together in the small breakfast nook and eating their soup and munching on cheese and crackers. Rain had told him she wanted to talk, yet they ended up eating in silence. It wasn't until they were clearing up the dishes that Joe turned to her.

"You said something about wanting to talk?"

Rain's heart jumped violently in her chest. "Yeah."

"Something on your mind?"

She carried the soup bowls to the sink. "Yes."

He followed her, carrying what remained of the crackers and cheese. "So, shoot."

She rinsed the bowls in the sink, slipping them into the dishwasher. "You know how much I appreciate everything you've done giving me a place to stay, giving me a job."

"Okay," he said slowly.

"And I don't think either one of us realized when I moved in here just how uncertain my prognosis was. My sessions with Dr. McGhan are going fine but it could be weeks, months, maybe even—" she stopped, taking a deep breath at the one thought that haunted her on a daily basis "—even years before I have any significant memory recall.

"Now I prefer to think of my recovery in terms of *weeks* instead of *years,* but the truth of the matter is, I simply don't know and because of that, it's unreasonable to think that our—our living arrangements could go on indefinitely, so—" she reached for a hand towel, twisting it between her damp hands "—so I really appreciate your hospitality, but I've decided to move out."

"*What?*"

His shocked, angry tone, surprised her.

"It's—it's not that I don't appreciate—"

"What do you mean you're moving out?"

"I just thought—"

"Where do you plan on going?" he demanded, cutting her off again.

"I thought I could get a place in town—"

"I suppose you want to leave your job, too," he said, accusing.

"Oh, no, I don't want—"

"Because if it's too much for you we can get someone in to help you."

"I don't want to quit my job," she insisted. "I love my job."

He stalked across the kitchen, stopping in front of her. He stared down at her, his chest heaving with emotion.

"Is this about last night?"

"What?" she gasped. "No."

"Last night was a mistake, I admit it," he continued, ignoring her protest. "I was out of line. It was inexcusable, I admit it. It was late, I'd had too much to drink, but I promise it will never happen again."

"Last night had nothing to do with my decision," she lied. It might be a big reason, but it wasn't the only one. "Things are so uncertain for me. I can't ask you to keep a roof over my head indefinitely."

"You're not asking," he insisted. "I'm offering."

"It's better this way."

"Better for who?"

"Whom," she corrected automatically, that fleeting feeling flicking through her consciousness again. "And it's better for both of us." She twisted the dish towel in her hands. "You've been wonderful, but I know it hasn't been easy for you, having me underfoot day in and day out."

"You're not underfoot."

She didn't want to argue the point, didn't want to hear what kind of explanation he had for all but ignoring her the last couple of weeks. His rejection had hurt, but there was no need for him to know that.

"Regardless," she said, dismissing the issue with a wave of her hand. "I think it's time for me to go."

He paced back and forth across the kitchen for a moment, running a hand through his long hair. "Where will you go?"

"I'm not sure yet," she admitted. "But Marcy is going to help me find a place."

"Marcy?" He stalked back across the kitchen toward her. "Marcy knows about this and didn't try to talk you out of it?"

Rain thought of all the reasons Marcy had given her on why she thought Rain should stay with Joe. Marcy had agreed to help only after Rain had convinced her that her mind was set.

"Marcy agrees I should do what I feel is best," she maintained, carefully skirting all the rest.

He stared down at her, his eyes dark and dangerous "And you think it is best?"

Looking up at him, Rain felt emotion grow thick in her throat. "I do."

For a moment she wasn't sure what he was going to do. The look in his eyes had gone from menacing to wild as his chest rose and fell with each rapid breath.

"No," he said shaking his head. Restless, he rocked back and forth, shifting his weight from one foot to the other. It was as if he were working up to something, as though something were seething inside, looking for a means of escape. "No, you can't."

This wasn't like him. He was normally so calm, normally played it close to the chest when it came to emotion. But there was nothing calm or restrained about him now. Maybe she should have felt afraid, or at the very least concerned. Instead, a thrill of excitement catapulted through her.

"Can't find a place? Yes, I can, I'm sure—"

"You can't leave."

The breath caught in her lungs. "I can't?"

"You can't," he said again.

"Joe, this is crazy. I have to. It's time. I have to go—"

"You can't leave!" he roared, grabbing her by the arms. The towel in her hands slipped and fell soundlessly to the floor. "I—I won't let you."

There was nothing unexpected or surprising about what he did next. He had grabbed her and hurled her against him, but at least a full minute passed before his mouth came crushing down on hers. In that moment, he had stared into her eyes and she had felt the depth and the breadth of the need in them.

He may have promised her he wouldn't kiss her again, but it was one promise he was destined to break. It was as if God and Nature had conspired to bring them together, to create between them a hunger so strong that neither caution nor common sense could control it. Whether it was right or wrong, wise or rash, prudent or foolish it was there and it was real and both were helpless to deny it any longer.

When he kissed her this time, she was ready for the onslaught, ready for the rush of fire and heat that hurled through her veins like lava from a volcano. Yet, the force of his kiss left her trembling. She didn't know if she'd ever been held by a man before, if she'd ever been kissed or desired or loved. She had been reborn by the desert, washed clean by the rain. What once had been was no longer. She had shed her past and walked into a future where there was only one man, one desire, one love.

"Rain," he murmured against her lips, his voice raw was need. "My Rain."

His hands slid down her arms, past her waist and

settled on her bottom. Pulling her tight, he pressed himself to her. He was hard against her and she felt herself grow weak.

She was as a virgin, unsullied, untouched, unadulterated, on a maiden voyage toward discovery. And yet in his arms, with his mouth on hers and his body desperately calling out to hers, all that seemed frivolous and unimportant. In Joe's arms, instinct took precedence over art, intuition over expertise. She became a woman on a mission, a woman whose only objective now was to please her man.

And he was her man. For this moment, Joe Mountain belonged to her and she to him. She clung to him, her mouth wild, her hands restless. She knew only too well how quickly everything could be snatched away, how in the space of a heartbeat one world could end just as another began and she wanted to grab up as much of Joe Mountain as she could. He was the world as she knew it, the sun, the moon, the past and the present. He was real, he was now and she wanted him more than she wanted back all that had been taken away from her.

"Rain," he growled. "I won't let you go. You're mine. You're mine."

He hauled her up, lifting her off her feet, his lips trailing a line of wet kisses along her neck and shoulder. The nightshirt had slipped up and somehow his hands had found their way inside, touching her bare skin.

She had no sensation of moving, no awareness they had moved until she felt edge of the counter against her back.

His hands were wild on her, moving beneath the nightshirt finding her thighs, her hips. In one smooth motion, he tore the shirt from her, his lips finding her breasts and savoring them.

When he lifted her up, she heard the sound of the dishes falling into the sink, felt the cold tile of the counter against her skin. She tugged at his shirt until blissfully it disappeared. She didn't know if she had torn it off or if he had taken it off, nor did she care. The only thing that was important was that her hands were free to move over him.

But soon that wasn't enough. She grew hungrier until the need in her threatened her very sanity.

"Joe."

His name tore from her lips like a plea for mercy. She was in pain, in dire need. She wanted him—madly, desperately, fervently. She could hardly think, could barely breathe. She had to have Joe Mountain, she had to or she wouldn't survive.

"Joe," she groaned again. "Joe, I want you."

The sound that came from his throat didn't sound human. It came from a more primitive time, from a more primal place. Like a hunter stalking his prey, his focus was on her to the exclusion of all else. He whispered something in her ear, strange, exotic-sounding words that seemed to float around her like a misty cloud, filling her lungs, her skin, her blood with an intoxicating vapor. It was a chant that told a story of nature, of creation and of the cravings of mind and body.

Frenzy became frantic. There was no time for seduction, no room for enticements and declarations. His mouth had savaged hers, and his hands had become lethal.

In a move that brooked no resistance, he pulled her to him, shoving into her in one, smooth stroke.

"Joe."

"Rain."

The names escaped into the mist around her, intertwining, coupling into the atmosphere. Her world had become a brilliant place filled with stars and moons and a sun of many faces, a place where time didn't matter and the past didn't exist. He had named her and now he had claimed her. She was Rain—*his* Rain—and he had become all elements to her. She didn't know who she'd been in the past, she didn't know who she would be in the future. But for now she was Rain and if ecstasy had a name it would be Joe.

There was an instant when the world had ceased to exist. In that millisecond of peace at the end of a heartbeat before the start of the another, all that there was had come to a halt in reverence. He was in Rain, and he had never known a pleasure so pure, so genuine, so absolute. What was happening was not only mind shattering, it was mind altering and Joe knew in that one, precious flash that he would never be the same again.

Within her he was whole, at one—with God, with Nature, with the universe of Man. He had found his way up and out of the underworld, had touched One Mother, had become new, reborn. He had found his place amongst the ancients, his place in the cosmos, the place he belonged.

The journey sent them both flying, climbing higher and higher toward that ultimate goal. He held on as long as he could, grasped at the last shred of reason, the last thread of sanity. But when he heard her cry of pleasure, when he felt her body wrench and writhe in ecstasy, he could restrain himself no longer. The end came in a radiant burst as he let himself go, freeing himself of the last vestiges of all that was tangible and was hurled into a vortex of bliss.

It was a long time before he could move, before sky and firmament took shape again and he was able to place the world around him. He didn't want to question what had happened, didn't want to think about cause or consequence. He just wanted to savor the moment, savor the feel of her in his arms.

He could feel her breath on his shoulder, could feel her heart beating against his chest and guilt tasted bitter in his mouth. She deserved to be pampered and indulged, soothed and placated and yet he had all but tossed her down and ravished her on the spot.

Gathering her close, he lifted her off the counter and into his arms.

"Wh-where are we going?" she murmured sleepily against his shoulder.

"To put you to bed," he said, moving through the house on legs that were less than steady.

She lifted her head, looking up at him. "Stay with me?"

She looked so beautiful something tightened in his chest. Leaning down, he kissed her.

"For as long as you want me."

They made love in his bed, the bed he had shared with Karen, the bed she had brought another man to. But all that didn't matter now. It was over, done with, long past. Now it was their bed—his and Rain's. They were together and that was all that mattered.

With the frenzy satisfied, with the hunger appeased, he was able to take time with her, to lure and to tempt her, captivate and seduce. She was like a flower, delicate and unique and yet there was a strength and a durability to her spirit that he could only admire. He touched her and kissed her, his hands playing across her beautiful body like a master musician with his favorite instrument. He urged her slowly, gently, profoundly to the final crescendo, needs playing louder and louder until form became frenzy and they burst together into the blissful void once again. Drifting, they floated together, hovering between sleep and wakefulness, wrapped in each other's arms.

He realized then it was time to face facts. With her in his arms, in his bed, he couldn't deny the truth that stared him right in the face. What he felt for Rain was more than admiration, more than desire and simple lust. Right or wrong, for better or for worse, he had fallen in love.

He'd tried to caution himself, had tried to temper his feelings and protect himself with the fact that someday she would recover her memories and return to the life from which she came. But his precautions had done little good.

Still, he couldn't find it in himself to regret any of it. The damage was already done. He loved her and even if that meant it had to end badly, he would savor what he'd been given and be grateful. He would be there for her as long as she needed him, even if that meant that someday he would have to let her go.

"Thank you."

He opened his eyes, gazing down at her and feeling her stir in his arms. "You're silly. What are you thanking me for?"

She closed her eyes, sighing deeply. "For this." She opened her eyes. "For everything."

He smiled. "This is very corny, but it was my pleasure."

She breathed out a small smile. "I hope it was—pleasurable for you."

He gathered her close, letting her feel his body's response to her nearness. "What do you think?"

She hesitated for only a moment. "I think I don't want you to have any regrets."

The small smile had faded from her lips and he saw the uncertainty in her eyes.

"None," he whispered with earnest. "Never."

"Are you sure?"

He leaned down, placing a small kiss on the tip of her nose. "I've never been so sure of anything in my life."

She sank down, pressing her face against his shoulder.

"But what about you?" he asked, wondering for a moment if she was laughing or crying. "How do you feel?"

She lifted her head, smiling up at him. "I feel wonderful."

Joe felt his heart swell in his chest. "Wonderful?"

"*Really* wonderful," she laughed.

"No regrets?"

She shook her head. "Not a one." Suddenly her gaze shifted then and she pointed to a spot on the front of his shoulder. "Well maybe just one."

In an instant, everything changed and his entire body tensed. He knew what was coming and braced himself. He'd been through it once before. "Yes?"

"It is with some regret that I'd never noticed this before. What is it?"

He glanced down to the spot on the front of his shoulder where her finger rested, to the small sun face surrounded by a moon and stars tattooed into his skin.

"A mistake," he confessed, remembering that night as a naive young sailor exploring his first foreign port after too many months at sea. He and five of his buddies from the ship had drank too much and thrown out one too many challenges. All six had awakened onboard the next morning hungover and tattooed.

She ran a finger over the design. "You don't like it?"

Her touch was light but it sent a jolt through him like an electrical shock. He'd been so caught up in the moment, so swept away by the emotions he'd completely forgotten about it, forgot about covering it or hiding it from her. He remembered all too well Karen's revulsion when she'd first seen the tattoo and how she'd made him promise to never let any of her family see it. Growing up on the reservation, he'd learned about prejudice and injustice, but it wasn't until he'd seen Karen's face when she'd looked at his tattoo that he'd learned about shame.

"A reminder of a momentary lapse in judgment that unfortunately I'll carry with me for the rest of my life," he said, glancing away. He didn't want to see the disgust in her eyes, didn't want to feel the shame.

"When you were in the navy?"

He nodded. "Young and stupid."

"I think we all do stupid things when we're young," she said philosophically, her finger tracing the outline of the tattoo again. "I'm sure I did." Grinning, she reached for his chin, turning his head until he looked at her. "And when I remember them I'll tell you all about them."

There was something so honest in her face, something so endearing and sincere it was all he could do to stop himself from taking her again. No judgment in her eyes, no disgust. It was only then that he realized just how tense and rigid he'd been holding himself. He'd been waiting for the other shoe to fall, for her to realize just what had happened and just what a mistake she had made.

"It—it doesn't bother you?" he asked, pulling her up to him.

She made a face. "Your tattoo? Why should it?"

He shrugged, feeling foolish now. "I don't know. I just thought maybe...you'd think it was...disgusting."

"Disgusting?" she repeated, pulling back and slipping down to look at the tattoo again. "Is there something nasty there I'm not seeing?"

Despite himself, he had to laugh. "No."

"Then why would I think it was disgusting?" She looked up at him and wiggled her brow. "Actually, I think it's kind of—" with her gaze still on him, she lowered her lips to the pigmented skin, slowly tracing the outline with her tongue "—sexy."

By the time he grabbed her up to him, he was trembling. With her simple act, she had torn away years of shame and regret and he realized what a fool he had been. It didn't matter that he had a tattoo. It was meaningless and unimportant. What was between them went beyond such trivialities.

"Thank you," he whispered after he'd kissed her long and deep.

"Now you're thanking me?" she murmured with a slow blink and looking just a little dizzy from the kiss. "What for?"

He shrugged. How did he tell her? How did he explain how much her oneness and acceptance meant to him, how much *she* meant to him?

"For being you," he said after a moment.

She started to say something, started to smile, but he stopped her with another drugging kiss. They made love again, their bodies melding together. There was nothing rushed now, nothing overlooked. Joe moved slowly and deliberately, taking time to touch, to savor, to explore and to cherish. Afterward, when they drifted asleep tangled in each other's arms, Joe floated on the clouds and dreamed of moons and stars and a sun with many faces.

The moon rose high in the sky, sending its milky glow spilling over the carpet and across the bed. Joe felt her body twitch, felt the perspiration bead along her skin.

"Logan."

The name was like an avalanche, destroying everything in its path, pulling him down from the cloud, back to the truth—a truth that was easier to ignore in the darkness. He was convinced that Logan was the key to all of this, that once he unlocked the mystery of Logan, all the pieces of Rain's puzzle would fall into place. But despite his best efforts, too many of those pieces lay scattered and lost.

She nestled close to him, the dreams that had disturbed her sleep over now, leaving her peaceful and still. He had no idea what time it was. Lying together, it was as if the world had stopped for them, as if time had ceased to exist and he wished it were in his power to make it stay that way. He wished the night would never have to end, wished the sun wouldn't come up and they would never have to face all the truths of the morning.

Tonight she belonged to him. Tonight they were just man and woman, Joe and Rain. She was in his bed, in his arms and under his skin. In the darkness they could pretend that nothing else was important, that there were no mysteries to be solved, no questions to be answered, and if he had the power to move heaven and earth, he would like to keep it that way.

If only there was a way things could stay the way they were right now, if it could always be unaffected and uncomplicated between them. But even as he felt her body stir beside him, he understood just how impossible that would be.

The sun would be up in a few hours and with the daylight would come the outside world and all its harsh realities. In the darkness, the outside world didn't matter; in the darkness he could pretend they belonged together, but soon that would all change.

She was a lost soul, a wandering spirit. Her past, her memories, her entire life had been snatched from her. It had been important to him from the first to find out what had happened to her and to restore her to her rightful life, but now, after tonight, it was more important than ever.

It was all right to dream, to fantasize and to make believe things could always be the way they were right now, but sooner or later he would have to face the dawn. With the sun came the realization that she couldn't remain his Rain forever. She needed her life back, needed questions answered. As long as Logan haunted her dreams, there would be no peace for either of them.

Chapter 11

"Wake up, sleepyhead."

Rain smelled the aroma of coffee and cinnamon even before she opened her eyes.

"What's all this?" she asked, squinting from the sunlight streaming in from the window to Joe standing in the doorway holding a huge silver tray in his hands.

"It's supposed to be breakfast in bed," Joe explained, carefully making his way toward the bed. "It's not very fancy, but at least you'll have something in your stomach." He set the tray down on the mattress beside her. "And we both know how cranky you get when you have an empty tummy.

Rain scooted up against the pillows, emotion feeling thick in her throat. His long hair fell loose around his shoulders and his broad chest rising above his flannel boxer shorts looked like carved mahogany. Rain didn't think she'd ever seen anything so beautiful.

"When did you do this?" she asked, clutching the

sheet up tight as she moved farther up to a sitting position. The morning paper leaned against the glass coffee carafe, which steamed with the fresh brew. A checkered napkin lined the small wicker basket, which brimmed with oversize cinnamon rolls.

Her entire system reacted to the smell of the coffee, helping her shake off the morning grogginess. But what had the lump of emotion in her throat swelling was the small vase filled with a few of the scrappy flowers that grew wild around the back doorstep.

"I didn't even hear you get up."

"Navajo," he said as he lowered himself to the bed. Leaning across the tray, he brushed a light kiss on her forehead. "We move like the wind."

She smiled up at him. "You're wonderful."

He rolled his eyes, reaching for the basket. "Here, eat something," he said, offering her a cinnamon roll. "I think you're getting light-headed."

She laughed, taking one of the rolls. But just as she started to take a bite, she caught sight of the clock beside the bed. "Oh, my gosh, look at the time," she shrieked, sitting straight up. "We're late!"

"Relax, it's Friday," he said, settling her back against the pillows. "You're taking a day off."

She looked up at him and blinked. "I am?"

"Yes, you are," he said firmly. Sitting down beside her, he reached for a cinnamon roll and took a bite. "And I am, too."

"Oh, yeah?"

He reached out, giving the tip of her nose a pluck. "Yeah."

She took a bite of her cinnamon roll, too. "Then how about pouring us a cup of that coffee?"

"Yes, ma'am," he said dutifully.

Rain leaned back and watched as he dutifully poured the coffee. Was it possible she'd ever been this happy before? Could she have known this kind of contentment, this kind of joy and forgotten it?

She thought back to their night together, of their long hours of lovemaking, the touching, the tenderness, the...

She swallowed, the bite of cinnamon roll landing in her stomach like a rock. It was hardly a realization, hardly a surprise. It was something she probably would have been aware of weeks ago if she'd dared to be honest with herself. She just hadn't wanted to admit it, hadn't wanted to believe it could be true. But after last night it seemed foolish for her head to keep denying what her heart already knew to be true. She had fallen in love with Joe Mountain.

"Cream and two sugars, right?"

"Right," she said, taking the cup from him.

He watched as she took a sip. "Okay?"

She smiled. "Delicious."

He leaned forward, plucking a quick kiss from her lips.

"You're right," he said with a grin, smacking his lips. "Now, what do you want?" He reached for the newspaper and leaned back against the pillows beside her. "Please, just don't tell me it's the sports page." He turned his head, giving her a wicked look. "I'd have to fight you for it."

"Don't worry, I'm not interested in the sports page," she assured him. "Or at least I don't think I am." She sat up, peering down at the paper he held. "Let me take a look."

"Oh, no, you don't," he said, shaking his head. "Here's your front page."

They both laughed as she took the paper and cuddled up next to him. The morning passed relaxed and lazy as they indulged themselves with all the things busy people are normally far too busy to do in the mornings. They pored through the newspaper, finding and reading quirky or interesting articles to one another, they poured second cups of coffee and nibbled slowly at their breakfasts, and they even flipped on the television, watching a morning talk show and then a soap opera, laughing and giggling as they tried to figure out the story line.

It was sometime after noon that Joe finally turned out of bed, grabbing Rain by the hands and pulling her up beside him.

"You know what I'd love to do this afternoon?" he asked, wrapping his arms around her waist.

"What's that?"

He tightened his hold, drawing her close. "I'd like to saddle up Sycamore and head for the boonies."

Rain's eyes widened, remembering Marcy's cryptic warnings of Joe's rustic mountain cabin. "The boonies! I've heard of that."

Joe grinned down at her. "From Marcy, I bet. She spent a pretty unforgettable Christmas there once. Did she tell you about that?"

"She's promised to tell me the whole story someday."

He lowered his head, brushing a kiss along her lips. "Come with me? We'll spend the night, have dinner, sit in front of the fire, come back in the morning."

"The boonies?"

He nodded.

"On a horse."

He nodded again. "You can ride Biscuit. You know how mellow he is."

She gave him a wary look. "How far is it?"

"We can be there in a couple hours." He jostled her in his arms. "Come on. You'll love it."

"The boonies on a horse," she repeated, as if saying it would help convince her.

He bent down and kissed her again. "We'll make love in a feather bed that's in the loft."

Apparently that was all the convincing she'd needed. "Okay," she said with a resigned sigh.

"Who knows," he said, kissing her again. "We just may end up staying the weekend."

Rain's eyes widened, hearing Marcy's warning in her head. "Okay, but I'm packing my own clothes."

If a few second thoughts crept into her brain as she neatly folded one of the new sweaters she'd bought and slipped it into the backpack Joe had given her, Rain did her best to ignore them. The day had been too perfect, being with Joe too wonderful for her to start questioning things now.

She knew better than most people just how uncertain life could be. What you had one minute could be snatched away the next. Like everyone, she faced an unpredictable future, but unlike the rest of the world, her past was just as unpredictable. Her road was a fragile one, her life a war between the past and the future. She couldn't afford cautious contemplations and long, drawn out designs. For her there was only here and now. With so much uncertainty, so much unknown, she didn't want to take any chances. She was determined to make the most of every moment of her time with Joe—now, while she could.

* * *

"Listen."

Joe lifted his head off the pillow, straining to hear. "I don't hear anything."

"There, listen," she whispered, her eyes widened. "Did you hear it?"

He listened again. His small, rustic cabin was remote, miles away from anyone or anything else. "Is that a bird?"

"An owl," she corrected.

He shook his head. "That doesn't sound like an owl."

"Trust me, it's an owl," she stated again.

They both froze as the sound broke the silence again.

"No," he insisted, pushing himself up against the pillow. "That's not an owl. That's more of a cooing."

"An owl," she said again. "A Burrowing Owl to be exact."

The song floated through the night again, sounding lonely and forlorn in the darkness.

"That's a dove," he insisted. "A mourning dove."

They looked at one another, the small loft lit only by the moonlight coming in from the skylight above.

"That's a Burrowing Owl," Rain said, listening to the gentle sound.

"I've never heard an owl coo."

She turned to him and grinned. "Well you are right now. The Burrowing Owl can make a monotone cooing sound that sounds very much like a mourning dove."

"Okay, Miss Smarty Pants," he said, plucking the top of her nose with his fingertip. "If it sounds just like a mourning dove, how can you be so sure it's an owl?''

"The pitch," she explained. "It's higher. Listen." As if on cue, the call sounded once more. Turning to him, she shrugged. "See?"

He was no expert on birds, but he did know what the coo of a mourning dove sounded like and she had a point—this did sound higher and had a harsher tone.

"An owl, huh?"

She nodded, letting him pull her close. "A Burrowing Owl."

He leaned down into the deep folds of the feather bed, pulling the quilt up around them. "You're full of surprises, aren't you?"

She looked up at him. "What do you mean?"

"First I find out you're practically an expert horse-woman, riding Biscuit up here like you were born in a saddle."

She made a face. "Oh, yes, just me and my saddle sores."

"Now it sounds like we've got a bit of an Audubon buff here, too." He leaned down and plucked a kiss along her mouth. "How did you get to know so much about birds?"

Looking back on it, he realized what a thoughtless thing that was, to ask such a pointed question and the look on her face when she realized she wasn't able to answer him was one he knew he would never forget. She looked up at him, her eyes round and tormented.

"Rain, please, I'm sorry," he said, reaching for her. "That was stupid. I wasn't thinking—"

"No, it's okay," she insisted, but the look on her face told him it was anything but okay. "It's—it's the strangest feeling. I mean, that's the call of a Burrowing

Owl—I know that.'' She looked at him, gesturing wildly with her hand. "I mean, Joe, I *know* that. There isn't a doubt in my mind.'' She stopped, drawing in a shaky breath. "The only problem is, I just don't remember how I know.''

The pain in her voice tore at him and he reached for her. She allowed him to pull her back into his arms, back under the covers, but after a moment she pulled back and looked up at him.

"You know,'' she whispered, her bottom lip quivering with emotion. "The first time you kissed me, you said it wasn't right—you and I being together, Joe. It isn't right.''

He reached down, running a hand along her cheek. "It feels pretty right to me.''

Her eyes filled with tears. "But I don't even know who I am. How do we know what happened out there in the desert? How can we be so sure I was the victim out there? If I'd been stranded or kidnapped or... assaulted—''

"Cruz already told you there were no signs of a sexual assault,'' he added quickly, interrupting her.

"I know, I know,'' she conceded. "But the point is, if I was the victim, why hasn't someone reported me missing? Why isn't there a family or friends or an employer looking for me? What if it turns out that I'm a criminal—an escaped convict or something?''

"Then I guess I'd have to read you your rights and turn you in,'' he said, refusing to be serious.

"What if it turns out when you find out who I really am, you won't...you won't—''

"Rain,'' he said, stopping her protest with a finger on her lips. "I may not know the name you were born with, I may not know where you come from or what

you do for a living, but I know who you are.'' He
brought her hand to his lips, placing a kiss into her
palm. ''I know your taste and your touch and how you
feel lying beside me. I know how soft your skin is,
how your eyes light up when you laugh and I know
how you make me feel and nothing—*nothing* is ever
going to change that.''

''I would hate it if you ever regretted—''

''Never,'' he whispered, stopping her with a kiss.

It was a long time before he felt her body relax,
before he felt her soft, rhythmic breathing and knew
she'd finally drifted asleep. It was only then that he
allowed himself to relax.

It haunted her. Every hour of every day, it haunted
her. All those things she didn't know, all those memories she couldn't remember, they were always there,
staring her in the face like a big black void. It didn't
seem to matter what she did or where she went, it was
always there and it haunted her.

She slept now, but there would be no true rest for
her, no real peace for either of them until they knew.
Maybe she never would fully recover from the amnesia, maybe she would never remember, but she still had
to know. She had to.

''One more time, Sheriff, pretty *please*.''

Joe looked into Annie Martinez's innocent little face
and melted. His shoulders ached from the ''horsey''
ride he'd just given her, but who could resist those
bright eyes and crooked smile?

''Oh, no, you don't, young lady,'' Marcy said before
Joe had a chance to answer. ''It's time for bed. You've
stalled around long enough.''

''But, Mommy—''

"No buts," Marcy warned, reaching for her daughter and lifting her down from Joe's shoulders. "Say good-night."

"Night," Annie said in a tiny voice. She reached up and gave Joe a hug, then ran across the living room and into her father's lap.

"Oh, no, you don't," Marcy warned when Annie snuggled under the protection of her father's arm. "Your father isn't going to save you this time. Into bed."

"Your mother's right," Cruz agreed, giving his daughter a hug. "Growing girls need their rest. Doctor's orders."

Frowning, Annie scrambled down from her father's lap and marched out of the room.

Marcy watched, rolling her eyes, then turned back to the men. "Would either one of you like some coffee after I get Annie down?"

Joe and Cruz looked at one another and then back to Marcy and nodded.

"So," Cruz said as he watched Marcy follow Annie out of the room. "Heard you took a few days off."

Joe turned around. "Word gets around this town fast."

Cruz laughed. "I went by the office the other day. Ryan told me." He paused for a moment, his gaze narrowing. "He also happened to mention Rain was gone, too."

Despite their close friendship, Joe felt uncomfortable. The four days he'd shared with Rain at his remote mountain cabin had been so wonderful and had meant so much, it was difficult to talk about. He'd never felt so free, so fulfilled, so complete as he had when he'd been with her. They'd hiked the mountain trails, cooked elaborate meals, sat up late into the night talking before a roaring fire, and made long, slow love in the loft on his feather bed. There were a million reasons why he never should have let it happen, why he never should have allowed himself to feel anything, to let things to go as far as they had and only one reason why he'd made the only choice he could. He'd never been so happy in his life.

He was in love and part of him wanted to shout it from the rooftops and part of him wanted to keep it all to himself, to hide it away from the rest of the world. He knew Cruz wouldn't judge him, wouldn't condone or condemn, but his feelings for Rain were still so new and their situation fraught with so many complications it made it difficult to talk about.

"Uh, yeah, we, uh, went up to the boonies for a few days."

"Oh, yeah? Get any fishing in?"

Joe's face felt flushed. "No, not really."

The was an awkward moment of silence, one where whatever unspoken message Joe had intentionally or unintentionally meant to communicate to Cruz about his reluctance to talk about Rain managed to hit its mark. Cruz nodded, changing the subject.

"So you said you had something you wanted to talk about?"

"Yeah," Joe said, settling himself into a chair across from Cruz. "I know you're not treating Rain any longer and I'm sure if McGhan thought this was a possibility he would have done it already, but I was just wondering about hypnosis."

"Hypnotizing Rain, you mean, in an effort to help her recover her lost memories?" Cruz summed up for him.

Joe shrugged and laughed. "Exactly."

Cruz smiled. "Hypnosis can sometimes be helpful, but it's not a cure-all."

"Do you think it could help Rain?"

"Hard to say," Cruz admitted. "There are a lot of things to consider, the least of which is the patient's susceptibility. Some people simply can't be hypnotized. And in all honesty, I'm sure if Mike McGhan thought it was right for Rain, he'd have used it by now."

"Has he said anything to you?" Joe asked. "I mean, does he send you any kind of report or anything?"

"Not really," Cruz said. "Rain is his patient now."

Joe let out a tired sigh and rubbed at his scratchy eyes. It had been stupid to think that the doctor treating Rain would have overlooked anything. He was just so frustrated, and felt so helpless because he didn't have anywhere else to turn.

"Yeah," he said, opening his eyes and drawing in a shaky breath. "I kind of figured it was something like that."

Cruz sat up, regarding Joe for a long moment. "I should probably give Mike a call, just check in and see how things are going."

"Could you do that?" Joe asked, perking up. "I'd— I'd feel better."

Cruz nodded. "No problem."

Joe gave his head a shake. "It's not that I don't think everything is being done, I was just hoping..." He stopped and gave his head another shake. "Grasping at straws."

"How is Rain doing?" Cruz asked after a moment

Joe shrugged. "She keeps up a front, of course, smiling and laughing, but I know she's troubled." He

leaned forward, resting his forearms along his thighs.
"And frankly, Cruz, I'm worried about her. The
dreams...they seem to be getting worse—nightmares
really."

"Does she remember much about them?"

"Bits and pieces, nothing specific." He sat back up,
pushing a strand of hair away from his face. "Except
Logan."

"Logan. The name she kept calling out the night
you brought her in."

Joe nodded. "She has dreams and she wakes up calling—'Logan, Logan, Logan.'"

"Logan?"

Both men turned as Marcy walked in, carrying a
small tray holding three mugs of coffee.

"Are we talking about Rain's Logan?" she asked,
handing Joe one of the steaming mugs. "Have you had
any luck with that?"

"Only bad," Joe admitted, taking the mug from her.
"I've run it through every Fed and state criminal database, name search, location search, missing person,
fugitive file, search engine and nothing." He stopped.
He took another sip, letting the coffee burn a path to
his stomach. "Plenty of Logans, just no leads." He
paused, taking a deep breath and trying to quell the
frustration that had him wanting to grab something and
break it. "I'm at a dead end here and I can't keep
going to her with nothing—I just can't."

Marcy walked over to him, putting a comforting
hand on his shoulder. "I think we've all seen how
difficult this is on Rain, but it hasn't exactly been a
picnic for you either, has it?"

"I don't care about that," he said in a quiet voice,
setting his cup on the table beside the chair. "I just

worry about her. She's trying, but it's tearing her apart inside.''

Marcy was thoughtful for a moment. ''You know, I still have a few friends at the attorney general's office in D.C. I'd be happy to give them a call if you think that would help.''

''Yeah, sure,'' Joe said quickly. ''That would be great.''

''I'll call first thing in the morning,'' Marcy assured him. She walked back to where Cruz sat, lowering herself down on to the arm of his chair. ''You know, I'd half expected to hear from Rain today. What's she up to?''

''She wanted to take Sycamore for a little ride,'' he said, remembering how he had watched her heading toward the stables as he drove down the drive. ''They've sort of formed a bond.''

She nodded, taking a sip of her coffee. ''Did she mention anything to you about wanting to find someplace in town?''

Joe stopped as he reached for his cup again. As much as he wanted to keep his relationship with Rain private, it was inevitable that it would come out. Besides, it was foolish to think Cruz and Marcy wouldn't put two and two together if they hadn't already.

''I think she's changed her mind about that.''

''Oh, really,'' Marcy said, giving Cruz an elbow in the arm. ''And why do you suppose that is, Sheriff?''

''I'm not sure, sweetheart,'' Cruz interjected, giving his wife a knowing look. ''But I think Joe and Rain might have discussed that very thing during their stay up in the boonies.''

Marcy's eyes widened as she looked from Joe to her

husband, then back to Joe again. "You and Rain went up to the boonies together—alone?"

"Okay, you two," Joe warned, rising to his feet.

"Something tells me he doesn't want to talk about this," Cruz pointed out.

"Joe Mountain," Marcy said in a stern voice. "Is there something you want to tell us?"

He smiled as he set his empty cup on the tray. "Believe me, Marcy, there is nothing I want to tell you."

"Maybe not," she conceded, rising to her feet. "But I think you've already said all you need to."

"Just watch that imagination of yours," he warned, turning around to give her a hug.

"I don't have to," she said, pulling back and looking up at him. "Everything I need to know is right there in your eyes."

The smile on his face faded. "Is it that obvious?"

"Just to those who know you," Cruz said, walking up behind Marcy. "Those who care about you."

"It's—it's hard to talk about."

"Then don't," Marcy suggested. "Just don't look so worried. It's not a tragedy, you know."

"I'm not so sure about that."

"Don't talk crazy," she said. "I think it's wonderful. You both deserve some happiness."

Emotion had his chest feeling tight and for a moment, Joe wasn't sure he could speak.

"But if I...if I don't find her past, we have no chance at a future."

"What are you doing out here?"

Rain stopped as she spread fresh hay around Biscuit's stall and turned around. "Hey, you. What are you doing home so early?"

"Looking for you."

She smiled, resting the pitchfork against the wall. "Well I like that."

Joe gestured with his chin. "So what are you doing cleaning stalls? Where's Charlie?"

"He's around somewhere. I'm just helping out." She turned and glanced behind her. "I'm just about through."

"Let me help," Joe said, coming into the stall and reaching for the pitchfork.

"I didn't think you'd be back until late," she said, slipping a hand on his shoulder while he worked and stretching up to give him a kiss on the cheek. "Don't tell me you missed me."

"Of course," he mumbled, a small smile breaking the harsh line of his lips. "Always."

It wasn't the sound of his voice or the expression on his face. It wasn't his stiff, awkward manner or his tight, clipped speech that had her blood turning cold and her stomach tying into a knot—it was all of those things.

"Joe, what is it? What's the matter?"

"Nothing's the matter," he insisted, tossing several more forkfuls of hay around the stall and leading Biscuit back inside. Slipping the pitchfork back on the hook on the wall, he turned to Rain. "But there is something we need to talk about."

"What is it? What's happened?" She heard the panic and the fear in her voice and did nothing to try to disguise it—she couldn't. She felt panicky and afraid.

"Come on," he said, taking her by the arm. "Come inside with me."

"No, tell me now," she demanded, stubbornly holding her ground and refusing to move. "Tell me what's wrong. What's happened?"

"Rain, we'd be more comfortable in the house—"

"Joe, tell me!"

He reached out, holding her by the upper arms, and drew in a deep breath. "I got a call today, a call that may be important." He dropped his hold on her, letting his arms slide to his sides and he took several steps back. "You know how I told you Marcy worked as a federal prosecutor in Washington before she married Cruz? Well, she still has friends in the U.S. Attorney General's office and last week I'd asked her to give them a call. I'd already checked all FBI criminal data banks but it was another resource to try, a place we hadn't tried before to get some information on your background or maybe some clue on figuring out what Logan is and..."

His hands balled into fists and he shifted his weight from one foot to the other.

"And what? My God, Joe, what?"

"Like I said, I got a call today." He drew in a shaky breath. "The U.S. Attorney General's office had been investigating a kidnapping involving a wealthy businessman in Philadelphia."

"What does that have to do with me?"

"I didn't think it did until I read the name. Logan Carvy."

"L-Logan!" she gasped, feeling herself grow cold all over. Her ears rang as the name echoed through her brain. Was this the Logan that had haunted her dreams and inhabited her nightmares and terrified her so? The name trembled from her lips. "He was kidnapped?"

Joe looked at her with eyes that would haunt her more than Logan ever had. He looked so hopeless, so overwhelmed, so sad. Was she a criminal after all? Had she been on the run, fleeing the authorities? Could reality be this cruel?

"No," he said, his voice cracking. "It was his...his wife."

Chapter 12

It was as if the ground beneath her had been violently shaken. She staggered back, crashing into the wall. He rushed to her, gathering her up into his arms.

She wasn't sure if she'd fainted, or if reality had once again become so impossible that she'd found a way to escape it, but whatever it was the next thing she knew she was sitting on the sofa in the living room and Joe was forcing her to sip from a glass of water.

"You just sit tight and rest for a moment," he said, putting the glass of water into her hand. "I'm just going to make a quick phone call—"

"Who are you calling?"

He reached up, pushing back a lock of hair that had fallen across her forehead. "I'm just going to give Cruz a call."

"No," she said, stopping him with a hand on his arm. "Don't call him. I'm fine."

"You don't look fine," he said, pressing his palm

along her forehead. "You're pale and I think you might be a little feverish."

"I'm not feverish. I'm fine," she argued, pushing his hand away. Struggling, she sat up, handing him back the glass. "Tell me what you've found out. I want to hear it all."

"Just let me call Cruz—"

"Joe!" she snapped, grabbed him by the wrist. He was stalling and she knew it, but she had waited long enough. "I want to know. I want to know all of it—*now!* What have you found out? Who am I?"

"All right, but keep in mind that none of this is certain, but—" he shrugged and began pacing slowly back and forth in front of her "—about eight weeks ago, the wife of a Philadelphia businessman named...Logan Carvy—"

"Oh, my God!" she gasped, her body going numb. She struggled to stand up. "Logan."

"Hold on, just wait a minute, wait a minute," he insisted, easing her back down on to the sofa. "Calm down. I'm not going to do this unless you promise me you'll stay calm."

Swallowing hard, she nodded her head. She wanted to say yes, wanted to tell him she'd make that promise, but she wasn't able to speak.

He hesitated for a moment, regarding her carefully before continuing. "Anyway, his wife had been abducted. The kidnappers kept him dangling for several weeks, making demands and threatening his wife's life if he went to the police. Eventually, a final ransom was demanded—a big one. Carvy got the money together and made the drop, but according to him, the kidnappers never made contact again after that.

"Carvy was reluctant to go to the authorities at first,

still fearful they'd harm his wife, but after waiting about a week, he called the police. He reported the crime just a few days ago, which explains why we hadn't picked up anything." Joe stopped pacing, walking to the sofa where Rain was sitting and kneeling down in front of her. "His wife's name is Rachel. Rachel Carvy."

"Rachel Carvy," she mumbled. Was that who she was? The name didn't sound familiar; it didn't sound like her. She'd thought when she'd finally found her name everything would feel right again, things would come back and make sense. But the name Rachel Carvy didn't sound right; Rachel Carvy didn't make sense. "But how could that be me? Why would I be found in Nevada?"

"Who knows? Mrs. Carvy had been missing for weeks, the kidnappers could have taken her anywhere in that length of time."

"But it still doesn't explain what happened out there in the desert."

"You're right, it doesn't."

"Then how can you be so sure this...Rachel Carvy could be me?"

"They sent me a description of the wife, of Rachel."

"And?" she prompted.

"It matched yours enough that I scanned your photos and e-mailed them a picture," Joe continued, reaching into the breast pocket of his shirt and pulling out a folded piece of paper. "And this is what they sent me back."

The image of the woman who had been digitized and reproduced on the laser printer wasn't the clearest, but she couldn't deny that it resembled her.

She glanced up from the photo, her lip quivering. "Is this me? Is this who I am? Am I Rachel Carvy?"

"We don't know anything for certain yet," he reminded her, reaching a hand out and running a finger along her cheek. "But it's something we need to check out."

"Wh-what do you mean?"

"I've made the arrangements. We're flying to Philadelphia in the morning," he said.

Rain felt nothing; she felt empty, void. This wasn't how it was supposed to be. This wasn't how she'd imagined it. She'd thought she would feel a sense of relief, a sense of purpose and direction once she finally knew. But now she just felt...numb.

"Rachel Carvy," she repeated. She looked up at him. "It means nothing."

"Nothing familiar? Not even Logan Carvy?"

"No," she said, shaking her head. He might as well be telling her she was Martha Washington for all the familiarity she felt. She had no more affinity for Rachel Carvy than she had for them. "What does she do, this Rachel Carvy, for a living I mean, did they tell you?"

"Carvy is wealthy from what I understand," Joe said. "His wife had been very active socially."

"A socialite? Is that what you're telling me? I could be a socialite?"

"Rain," he said, taking her by the arms. "Let's just take this one step at a time right now. We don't know anything for certain. Let's get to Philadelphia, see how you feel about things then."

"How I feel about things," she repeated, pushing his arms away and sitting up. "I can tell you how I feel about things—I feel nothing. How can that be?

There's a chance I'm this socialite Rachel Carvy and I feel nothing.''

She stood up, pushing past him and walking to the window. ''What if...what if we don't go?''

''What do you mean? We have to go.'' He started across the room toward her.

''Do we?'' She whirled around, facing him.

''Of course we do, Rain. This could be your life, your past. We can't just turn our backs on that.''

''Can't we? I don't know who this Rachel Carvy is. The woman is a stranger to me, her husband is a stranger to me.'' She reached out, grabbed at him. ''I'm Rain now, Joe. What happens to that? What happens to us?''

She knew she wasn't making any sense, knew that what she was saying was impossible, but she didn't want sense and reason right now. She was too frightened, too unsettled.

She had longed for the day she would remember, longed to know who she was and where she'd come from. But now, now that it looked as though the mysteries of her past were finally to be solved, all she could think about was how much it was costing her.

''Rain, you're talking crazy,'' he insisted, reaching out for her. ''You're just feeling a little overwhelmed right now. This is what we've been waiting for, the first solid lead that's going to put an end to this, once and for all.''

''But that other life, those other people, they're strangers to me. I don't know them, I don't remember them.'' She clutched at him, feeling more desperate, more frightened than she had that day in the desert. ''This is where I belong, Joe. This is where I want to be.'' She pulled back, looking up at him. "I'm Rain now. And this is where I belong—here, with you.''

He let her cling to him, let her kiss him and hold on to him tightly, but when he looked down at her, his face was grave and full of dread.

"Rain, this isn't just about you and me." He carefully freed himself from her embrace, taking several steps back. "There are other factors to consider, other people involved."

"I don't care," she insisted boldly. "This is my life now and I don't want to give it up. I don't want to go back."

"Rain, you have to," he said, his voice hoarse with emotion. "There are..."

There was something in his eyes when he looked at her, something dark and utterly hopeless, something that turned her blood to ice.

"Rain," he continued. "There are children. Rachel Carvy is the mother of two children."

Rain staggered back, her legs buckling beneath her. Tottering, she landed against the cushions of the sofa, too dazed to do more than stare up at him.

"Ch-children?" she stuttered.

Joe walked back across the living room, kneeling once more in front of her. "A boy and a girl."

"Children," she mumbled again. "A son. A daughter."

"These children have been without their mother for the last eight weeks," he said, gathering her hands in his. "Rain, you owe it to them—you owe it to yourself to find out if you're their mother." He squeezed her hand. "Come with me tomorrow to Philadelphia. Come with me to find out if you're Rachel Carvy."

Even though everything in her wanted to revolt,

wanted to run and hide and not think about any of this again, there had never been any real question in her mind whether she would actually go with him or not. Of course she would go—she had to. She had to know one way or another if this was who she once had been.

She tried to picture herself married, the wife of a wealthy businessman, a mother of two children. It seemed unfathomable to her that she could be this person—this Rachel Carvy. How could she have forgotten the man she loved? How could she have forgotten her children?

"I'm scared, Joe," she confessed.

"I'm scared, too," he admitted.

"Joe, I—I don't want to lose you, Joe."

"You never will, " he whispered.

The emotion in his voice had tears springing into her eyes. Even if it turned out that she wasn't Rachel Carvy, there was a life out there where she had once belonged. And it wasn't until this moment, it wasn't until she'd been given so much hope for discovering her past that she realized how much she was going to lose.

"I came as soon as I heard," Marcy said, rushing through the front door and throwing her arms around Rain's neck. "Are you okay?"

For a moment Rain couldn't speak. The emotions were simply too strong, too overwhelming. They rendered her speechless. She simply stood there, clinging to Marcy and feeling tears well up in her eyes.

"I don't know what to feel." Marcy confessed after a moment, tears streaming down her cheeks, too. She pulled away. "I'm happy for you, I am, I guess.

You've waited so long and you need to know. It's just…''

"I know," Rain said, her voice thick with emotion. "I'm not exactly sure how I'm suppose to feel, either—happy, sad, scared?" She took Marcy's jacket and hung it over a hook on the hall stand, then walked with her into the living room. "Of course, it's all speculation at this point, nothing certain, but we're leaving for Philadelphia in the morning."

"So soon?" She sat down on the sofa beside Rain.

"I know," Rain said with a sigh. "I'm having a little trouble believing it myself. It's all happening fast."

"I was hoping…" Marcy reached out, taking Rain's hand. "I don't know, I guess I was hoping we'd have a little more time."

Rain stared down at Marcy's hand on hers and felt choked by emotion again. Suddenly she was crying once more, tears blurring her vision and spilling onto their hands.

"Oh, Marcy," she sobbed. "What's the matter with me? I thought once I knew it would be so wonderful, I thought it would be so much better, but now…now I'm just scared."

Marcy wrapped her arms around Rain, rocking her gently. "I know sweetie, I know."

"I don't want to go," she confessed tearfully. "I know that's awful, I know that's a terrible thing, but I can't help it."

"It's okay," Marcy said, in a soothing voice.

It was a long time before the emotions had spent themselves and Rain felt in control again.

"I'm sorry," she sniffed, pulling a handful of tissues from the pocket of her jeans. "I don't know what's happening to me. I've been so...so emotional since this whole thing started.'' She wiped at her tears. ''I mean, nothing's certain, right? This could all just turn out to be nothing. Joe and I could get out there and find out I'm not who they think I am at all and we can come home again.''

Home. Suddenly the word had a sad, melancholy sound. *Home.* This had been her home—this town and the people in it, this house and the man she had shared it with. This was her home—the only one she'd ever known, the only one she wanted. Would all that change when she entered the world of Rachel Carvy?

''Of course,'' Marcy agreed. ''You're just going to check things out.''

''Right,'' Rain said, taking a deep breath. But the optimism was false and they both knew it. ''Oh, Marcy,'' she said with a sigh. ''How can I be this person they think I am? A husband and children—how can that be? How could I forget a husband? How could I forget my own children?''

''You suffered a trauma. You have amnesia,'' Marcy reminded her. ''That's what happens when you have amnesia—you forget.''

''But it's like hearing about strangers. There's nothing familiar, nothing jogging my memory. It's like I'm hearing about characters in a book or in a movie. They don't feel real to me.''

''Well, once you get to Philadelphia that'll change. Once you put faces to these people you'll feel differently.''

Rain turned to her and smiled. ''You're right. Thank you.''

''Of course I'm right,'' Marcy joked, smiling. ''I'm a judge. Judges are always right.'' But after a moment, her smile faded. "I know you're going to be busy, but you have to call and tell me what's going on, promise?"

"I promise," Rain vowed.

"No matter what happens."

Rain nodded. "Okay."

"Even if it's just a false alarm, okay?"

Rain had to smile. "Even if it's just a false alarm, I promise."

Marcy drew in a deep breath. "I'm going miss you—we all are." She hesitated for just a moment. "Especially Joe."

Rain turned away. Leaving Joe was something she couldn't even think about yet. It was all happening so fast—too fast. She'd been caught in a storm, swept up in a gale of speculation and guesswork that left her feeling dazed and confused. She didn't know what to think, didn't know what to feel, but facing it all without Joe wasn't something she could even consider at the moment.

Maybe once she knew for certain she'd feel differently. Maybe once she remembered the love a wife had for her husband, the love a mother had for her children, maybe then the thought of not having Joe in her life wouldn't seem so terrifying, but she couldn't even fathom that now. It hurt too much to think about saying goodbye to him, about not seeing him or being with him every day, not talking with him, or touching him, or hearing his voice. How was she going to survive? How could she let him go?

"I know I'm going to miss all of you," she whispered.

"Especially Joe," Marcy added again.

Rain knew she was crying again, only this time she

wasn't sure she would ever be able to stop. "Especially Joe."

Marcy hugged her tight.

"I know it wasn't right," Rain confessed. "I never should have let it happen until I knew who I was, but I couldn't help it." She pulled back, looking into Marcy's caring brown eyes. "I love him, Marcy. How am I ever going to be able to let him go?"

"I'm glad Marcy came by."

Rain nodded, watching as the taillights of the car disappeared into the darkness. Stepping back inside the house, she closed the front door. "She's been a good friend."

Joe nodded. It had been one hell of a day and they would have to leave early in the morning to get to Reno in time to make their plane. But he was too keyed up, too restless to think about going to sleep. Besides, there would be plenty of time later to think about those mundane necessities of life, after he came back from Philadelphia, after he'd said goodbye to Rain.

He stepped to one side, letting her pass, then followed her down the short corridor and into the kitchen. He still wasn't sure how he was going to do it, how he was going to stand to the side and watch her walk away, watch her walk into the arms of another man.

He'd downplayed it for Rain, letting her believe there was a possibility she wasn't Rachel Carvy, but gut instinct told him there wasn't a doubt. She was Mrs. Logan Carvy—wealthy wife, mother and definitely not his.

Of course, if he'd have been smart he would have forced himself to stay away, forced himself not to want her, not to touch her. After all, he'd known from the beginning there had been another life out there some-where, another place where she belonged, another man who longed to have her back. If he had been smart, he would have kept reminding himself there could never really be a future for them, that what there was be-tween them would have to come to an end once she'd discovered that other life again. If he had been smart...

Smart. That was the problem. He hadn't been smart since he'd laid eyes on her. He'd broken every rule he'd ever made for himself, breached his own common sense and violated every good intention. It wasn't as though he hadn't seen it coming—he had, he just hadn't done anything to stop it. He'd wanted her—from the first, from the beginning. He'd walked into this whole thing with his eyes wide-open, blinded by desire, blinded by...

No, he wasn't going to say the word, he wasn't even going to think it again. It had no place in his life, no room in his head. He'd dropped his guard, let his heart take control and now he's paying the price. This was his Armageddon, his day of reckoning and the time to let go.

"Are you hungry?" he asked, walking to the refrig-erator and pulling the door open. "I could fix you something."

Rain shook her head. "No, thanks."

"You sure?" he asked, bending down and aimlessly surveying the contents inside. He wasn't hungry and he knew she wasn't, either; but since sleeping was out of the question, cooking would at least give him some-thing to do. And that's what he needed, something to do, something to fill in the time and the space until he had to let her go. "How about some scrambled eggs?"

She started to shake her head then stopped, thinking better of it.

"Well, why not?" she said, pushing herself to her feet and heading across the kitchen toward him.

He grabbed for the eggs as she reached around him for the cheese and milk and they quietly went about the job of fixing their meal. He didn't doubt for a moment that hunger was not what was motivating her any more than it was motivating him. She was looking for something to fill up the time, too.

"Should I make toast?"

"Sure," he said, thinking toast would probably go good with the eggs they weren't going to eat anyway.

Unfortunately, the meal didn't take nearly long enough to finish and before he knew it, they were sitting opposite each other in the breakfast nook in front of a platter of eggs and toast neither of them wanted.

"You're not eating," he said, watching her push the eggs around on her plate.

Rain looked down at her plate, then back up to him. "I guess I'm not as hungry as I thought I was."

He looked down at his own untouched plate. "I know what you mean."

And so they sat there, neither making any move to leave or to eat, or do anything other than stare down at their plates, lost in their own thoughts.

"What if I don't remember them?"

He looked up. "Rain, don't think about that."

"I can't help it," she confessed. "What if I don't? If I'm who they think I am, what if I don't remember those people when I see them—my children, my..." She stopped, her voice failing. She swallowed hard and cleared her throat. "My husband. What if I don't remember them?"

"Let's just wait and see how you feel once you get there."

"I know, I know," she conceded impatiently.

"And besides, you might feeling differently once you get there."

"You're assuming I'm going to walk off that plane and everything's going to come back." She sat up, a false smile on her face, and raised her hand in a waving motion. "Hi, everyone, here I am. Mommy's back!" she mocked. "What if that doesn't happen? What if I don't remember them?"

"Then you get to know them again."

She stood up, walking to the window. Closing her arms around herself, she stared out into the blackness of the night.

"You'd leave me there? With strangers?"

"Why are we talking about this now? Let's just wait—"

"I don't want to wait," she snapped, turning around. "I'm tired of waiting." Her arms dropped to her sides. "I want to know now, Joe. Would you leave me there, with people who were strangers to me?"

He leaned back in his chair. "Rain, what are you doing?"

"I'm just curious, that's all."

He shrugged. "What do you want me to say?"

"I want you to tell me if this is upsetting to you, that you wished it wasn't happening," she insisted, emotion making her breath come in rapid, short bursts. "Or maybe it's not such a bad thing. Maybe it's convenient for you."

He frowned, coming forward in his seat. "Convenient? What are you talking about?"

"Let's face it, Joe, you and I have been going pretty

hot and heavy lately," she explained with a humorless laugh. "And this couldn't have come at a better time if you'd been having any second thoughts or—"

He wasn't sure what she said after that. He could see where she was going with this line of reasoning and all he could see was red. He stood with such force, his chair fell backward, landing on the hardwood floor with a horrific crash.

"All right, that's enough," he demanded, stalking toward her. His chest was rising and falling with emotion and he wasn't sure if he wanted to grab her and shake her or drag her into his arms. "I don't know what you're trying to do or trying to get me to say, but let's set the record straight on one thing. If you think this is convenient for me, it's not. If you think this is easy for me, it's not." How was he supposed to make her understand how difficult that was going to be for him? "Rain, if it turns out that you are Rachel Carvy, those people—those strangers—are your family, whether you remember them or not." He walked to where she was standing, putting a hand on her arm. "What would you want me to do, take you away? Would you really want to leave them again?"

Rain crumpled, her head dropping to her chest. "I don't know."

He reached down, slipping a finger under her chin and tilting her head back until she looked up at him. "Yes, you do."

She nodded, sighing heavily. "Maybe I do."

"Of course you do, because it's the right thing."

She looked up at him, her face sad and unhappy. Her eyes were dry. There would be no more tears. She'd cried all she was going to, resisted all she could.

The inevitable was upon them, and now it was time to accept.

"The right thing," she whispered. "But it doesn't feel right, Joe. It feels wrong. Leaving you feels wrong."

He stared down at her, feeling something tighten in his chest. The reality of what was happening couldn't be ignored, couldn't be pushed aside or swept under the rug. It was right there, staring them both in the face. Tomorrow would change their lives forever. Tomorrow he would return her to another life, another family, another man. She would stop being Rain and become Rachel Carvy—Mrs. Logan Carvy. She would have wealth, society, a husband and a family and no room in her life for a Navajo sheriff from an out-of-the way place like Mesa Ridge. He had less than twenty-four hours to find a way to walk away from her and never look back.

He pulled her close. Tomorrow she would be Rachel, but tonight she was still Rain, and Rain would always belong to him.

"Rain," he whispered, cupping her face in his hands and brushing his mouth to hers. "How does this feel?"

"Oh, Joe," she groaned, pressing her lips to his. "I love you, Joe. I love you."

Even as he crushed her mouth to his, her words vaporized into the air around them, drifting like a thick, intoxicating cloud that seeped into his bloodstream making him feel light-headed and dizzy.

Love. How he wanted to believe her, how he wanted to forget about cautions and controls and doing the right thing and celebrate the fact that she loved him. And he didn't doubt for a moment that she had meant what she said; he just couldn't allow himself to believe it. Her world was too new, her realm of experience too limited for her to know about what it was she felt. She relied on him, depended on him, needed him and it was just too easy for her to confuse those things with love.

But he wasn't confused. His world wasn't new. It had begun before time, before there was day or night, before First Woman had led the chosen people up from the underworld, before they had felt the warmth of the sun or pondered the glow of the moon. There was a time when he'd been mistaken about love, when what he'd thought was love had turned out to be desire and flattery—and even envy. But from the moment he had seen Rain, his feelings had been crystal clear. It was love; he'd recognized it from the beginning, understood it, and hadn't confused it with anything else. He was in love with her—in love with Rain.

"Make love to me, Joe," she moaned against his lips. "Here, now. Please." She pressed her mouth to his again. "Please."

Didn't she know that's just what he wanted to do? Didn't she know he wanted her—right here, right now, while she was still in his arms, while she was still Rain and still belonged to him? He wanted to carry her up the stairs, up to his bed and never wanted to let her go. But he couldn't do that—he wouldn't.

He had broken a lot of rules since he'd met her—rules about wanting and needing, rules about touching and allowing himself to feel something even though he knew it wasn't right.

And it wasn't right. Even though everything in him wanted to argue the point, the truth stood between them and the truth was, she no longer belonged to him—she never had. She was Rachel Carvy and she belonged somewhere else and to someone else. He wanted her, he loved her, but she could never be his.

"Rain," he groaned against her lips. He almost thought it would have been easier to relieve Atlas of his task of shouldering the weight of the world than it would be to push Rain away, but that was exactly what he had to do. "Rain, no."

"Joe," she murmured again, clutching at him.

"Rain, please," he pleaded, putting his hands on her shoulders and struggling to set her away. "No, Rain, we…we can't. Rain, stop."

The word cut through the haze of desire and longing, through the mist of need and hunger. Dropping her hold on him, she stepped back, eyes opening wide.

"You want to stop?"

"We have to stop," he insisted, his grip on her arms tightening as though sensing a struggle. "We can't do this. I—I can't do this."

She struggled free despite his hold on her arms. "Can't?" she asked. "Or won't."

His arms dropped to his sides. "What does it matter? We can't do this, you know that. It's not…not right."

"The right thing," she sighed, turning away. "We're back to that again."

"Because we're the kind of people who do the right thing."

She spun back around. "But couldn't we just forget this one time?"

He reached out, running the backs of his fingers along her cheek. "That's not possible and you know it."

"Do I?" She looked up at him, her eyes pleading. "Joe, we may never be alone like this again. This could be our last night together—our last chance.

Couldn't we just forget about doing the right thing this once?''

"It's because this could be our last night together that we have to do what's right,'' he explained, the look in her eyes one he knew would haunt his dreams for a long time to come. "Tomorrow I have to turn you over to another man. If we're together tonight, I'm not sure I'd be able to do that.''

Chapter 13

Joe glanced down at his watch. Logan Carvy was due at FBI headquarters at six o'clock and it was nearly seven now. Where the hell was he?

Looking up, he stared out the window of the highrise office building at the glow of the city lights below. The pressure at his temples tightened, throbbing painfully. He didn't want to dislike Logan Carvy, didn't want to resent the man, but the guy was taking it awfully easy. The man was getting his wife back from the dead, for heaven's sake. You'd think the least he could do was be on time.

Joe thought of Rain waiting back at the hotel. She'd been exhausted when they'd gotten off the plane this afternoon. She'd been up most of the night before and he knew she hadn't gotten any sleep on the plane. He'd waited at the hotel until she'd gotten settled in her room before leaving for this meeting. He hoped she would be able to get some rest, but knowing her the way he did, it seemed unlikely that would happen. She was too wound up, too nervous to settle down.

He looked down at his watch again and swore under his breath. What was it with this guy? Where the hell was he? What could be more important than this? Granted this was just a preliminary meeting and Carvy knew Rain wasn't going to be there, but did that mean it was okay for him to keep them waiting?

Joe turned away from the window, pacing back and forth and stretching the taut, tense muscles of his neck and shoulders. He felt restless, edgy and couldn't shake a nagging sense of uneasiness that had been bothering him since they stepped off the plane three hours ago. Maybe he was just looking for trouble, looking for anything to find fault with, but his Navajo blood was telling him that something was amiss, something wasn't right.

Carvy had been made aware from the beginning of Rain's amnesia and had agreed to meet with Joe and local FBI agents alone first to formally identify photographs of Rain and to clear up details of the kidnapping and ransom demands. If Carvy did formally identify Rain as his wife, as they all expected him to do, a meeting had been planned for in the morning at the Carvy house where Rain—or, rather, Rachel—could be reunited with her husband and family in the privacy of their own home.

Joe walked back to the window and stared out into the night. So where was Carvy? Why wasn't he here counting the moments until he could hold her again?

Joe closed his eyes, shutting out the city lights. If she were his wife, he wouldn't have let anything stop him. He would have been at the damn airport waiting.

He opened his eyes. But Rain wasn't his wife—she

wasn't even Rain any longer. She was Rachel Carvy and it was his job to return her to her husband—if the guy ever decided to show up.

"I'm going to try to get someone on the line, try to find out what the holdup is."

Joe turned to Neal Rubin, sitting at the conference table in the middle of the room. The seasoned FBI agent looked as frustrated as he felt.

"That probably wouldn't be a bad idea," he agreed, stepping away from the window. "We probably should find out if there has been some kind of mix-up."

"There's been no mix-up." They both looked at the sound of the door opening. "I'm Logan Carvy."

The tap on the door was so quiet she barely heard it, but nerves had her reacting as though it had been as loud as an explosion.

She leapt off the bed and ran across the room, squinting to peer through the peephole in the door. Despite the distortion of the glass, Joe's handsome face looked somber and serious.

"Good, you're still up," he said when she opened the door. "Could I come in for a minute?"

"I didn't think you'd ever get back," Rain said, stepping to one side to let him pass. "I've been going crazy waiting." She closed the door behind him and followed him into the room. "What took so long? What happened?"

"Well, I met with Logan Carvy," he announced in a tired voice, walking to the table and chairs near the window.

Logan. Rain shivered. If this was the name of her husband, why did it still send a chill rifling through her, leaving her feeling cold and numb?

"Y-you did?"

He pulled one of the chairs from the table and collapsed into it. Sighing heavily, he nodded.

Logan. This was the man who was supposed to be
her husband, the man she loved, the man she shared
two children with. So why did his name still fill her
with dread? Why did it make her shake? Why had it
tortured her dreams and left her feeling frightened and
alone?

She wandered to the table and reached for the other
chair, sitting across from him. "Wh-what was he
like?"

Joe leaned forward, resting his elbows on the table,
and rubbed at his eyes. In all the weeks that she had
known him, she'd never seen him look tired, but he
looked tired now. In fact, he looked utterly exhausted.

"I don't know," he said with a shrug. "He's not
very tall, but broad shouldered, dark hair." He pushed
himself away from the table, leaning back in the chair.
"He didn't have horns or a tail or anything like that."

She leaned back then, too. She wasn't sure if he was
trying to be funny or not, but she could find nothing
humorous in any of this.

"So what...what happened? What did you talk
about?"

Joe sighed again. "You mostly—where you were
found, your injuries. There was talk of the kidnapping,
about the demands that had been made, things like
that." He thought for a moment, then shrugged.
"That's pretty much all."

She drew in a deep breath. It was as if they were
talking about someone else, about a character in a
movie or a book—but they weren't. They were talking
about her.

"You took pictures...of me. Did you show them to him?"

Joe came forward in his chair again. "Yes, I did."

"And...?" She held her breath, but the answer really was no mystery to her. She could see it on Joe's face, in every move that he made.

"And he identified you," Joe said in a flat, dry voice. "As his wife."

Rain felt a little like she'd been hit hard in the stomach. Even though she had known what the answer would be, hearing it still brought a reaction. She hadn't realized until that moment that she had been holding her breath, that she had been holding herself rigid, bracing every muscle for the blow.

"You okay?" he asked after a moment.

Actually, she thought she was going to be sick, thought she was going to throw up all over everything, but she didn't. Instead, she nodded, and rose slowly to her feet, her legs feeling shaky and unsteady beneath her.

"So, I guess that's it then. No more guessing, right?"

He nodded, turning away. "Looks that way."

"So, uh, where do we go from here? Am I going to have a chance to meet my husband or are you just going to drop me off at...home?"

He didn't react to her sarcasm. "We've set up a meeting at Carvy's house in the morning."

A chill sent a shiver rattling through her, leaving her teeth chattering. For the second time in less than forty-eight hours, she had reason to dread the dawn of a new day.

"I see," she murmured, wondering how she was ever going to make it through another long night. She took several unsteady steps away from the chair. "Did he…uh, Logan, I mean. Did he say anything? About me, I mean?"

Joe pushed himself away from the table and stood up, too. "I told you, we talked about the abduction—"

"That's not what I mean," she snapped, cutting him off. "Did he say anything about…about me, about finding me, about me being here, about…wanting to see me?"

Joe walked up behind her and for a moment she thought he was going to pull her into his arms. That's what she wanted him to do, that's what she needed— to feel his strong arms embracing her, to feel his strength, his warmth, his support. But he didn't reach out, he didn't make any move to touch her at all, and another icy shiver shuddered through her.

"I think he's anxious to have his wife back, if that's what you mean."

"Good," she said, forcing the word out of her mouth. She walked to her suitcase, which lay open on the bed. "So I guess it's probably not a good idea to unpack, since it looks like I will be going…home in the morning."

"Rain, don't—"

"Rachel," she corrected, turning back to him. "Might as well start getting used to it."

He stood there for a moment, looking at her, his expression taut and stiff. "Whatever you like."

What she liked? What she liked was the name Rain and the way he would say it.

"The children," she said quietly. "You didn't say but I assume they weren't there."

"No, they weren't there," he assured her.

"Did he, Logan, I mean? Did he mention anything

about them, about the children? Will they be there in the morning?''

''No, they won't be there.''

She looked up, surprised. ''No?''

Joe shook his head. ''He said he thought it would be better if the two of you had…'' He paused for a moment, swallowing hard. ''If the two of you had some time alone together first.''

''I guess that makes sense,'' she conceded, trying to imagine what that first meeting would be like. How was she supposed to greet the husband she didn't know? Did she shake his hand, run into his arms? ''And it's probably the best thing for the children, too.'' She reached down and flipped closed her suitcase. ''Did he say anything about them? How they were, if they knew about me?''

''We really didn't talk that much about them,'' he said, turning around and walking back to the table and chairs. ''He said he hadn't wanted them to get their hopes up until he knew for sure.''

''I see.''

He shrugged. ''I guess it's only natural he'd be protective of them. He did mention their names, too, and I'm sorry I can't remember—''

''Christian and Robyn.''

He stopped and slowly turned around. ''What?''

It was only then that she realized what she'd said, that she realized what had just happened.

''They are Christian and Robyn,'' she said, as the world swayed and tilted around her. ''Christian is nine and Robyn eight.''

''Rain, what are you saying?''

She staggered forward a step. She couldn't explain what had just happened. She'd had no warning, no no-

tice. She'd just opened her mouth and the names had
been there—names and faces. In the space of a breath,
everything had changed. What she hadn't known a moment earlier, she knew with certainty now. And just as
the door to her memory had opened, so did the door
to her heart. Love swelled in her chest.

"Christian," she said, whispering the name again as
the picture of a bright-eyed, curly-haired boy formed
in her mind. "He plays soccer and hockey and is a nut
for video games." She lifted her gaze to Joe, feeling
a sense of wonder she hadn't known existed. "And
Robyn has long, thick red hair and gets straight As and
loves to ride her bike."

Joe ran across the room to her, clutching her to him.
"You remember."

It wasn't until she felt the tears on her cheeks that
she realized she was crying. "I remember." She
grabbed at him. "Oh, God, Joe, I remember them."

"What else, Rain?" he asked after a moment.
"What else do you remember?"

Looking up, she saw the tears in his eyes, too.
"They're not his children."

"What?"

"Christian and Robyn," she said, feeling herself
growing cold all over. "They're not Logan's natural
children. They're his stepchildren."

"Stepchildren?"

"Stepchildren! What's this about stepchildren?"

Joe heard Marcy's startled question in the background.

"Joe says Rain remembered that Logan Carvy is her
children's stepfather," Cruz said in a muffled voice,
relating the news to his wife.

Joe rubbed at his scratchy eyes as he listened. It was nearly three in the morning Philadelphia time, making it around midnight in Mesa Ridge, but the message from Cruz and Marcy he'd had waiting when he'd finally gotten back to his room had asked that he call whatever the hour.

After her startling recollection, Rain had been too keyed up to sleep, too emotional to settle down. He had sat with her for several hours comforting her as best he could. She had been so overwhelmed by all of this, so dismayed it had broken his heart. Too much was happening too fast and she was near the breaking point. What he'd wanted was to take her into his arms, to hold her and kiss her until all of this disappeared, but of course that had been out of the question. Instead, he had sat with her, holding her and doing what he could to help her adjust and accept.

"Ask him how Rain is? Is she okay?" He could hear Marcy's voice in the background.

"Marcy wants to know—"

"I heard," Joe said, stopping Cruz with a stifled yawn. "And tell Marcy she's okay. Tired, of course, but I think she'll sleep tonight. She was exhausted when I left."

"And she'll be meeting with this Logan Carvy in the morning?"

Joe felt something go tight in his stomach. "That's the plan."

"So you met this guy, this Logan," Cruz said. "How'd that go?"

"Okay, I guess."

"So what's he like?" Cruz prodded.

Joe closed his eyes and thought of the short, stocky man who was Rachel Carvy's husband. He realized there was no way he could judge the man fairly—he was married to the woman he loved! That alone was reason enough not to like the guy. Still, he had tried his best to put all that aside, tried not to let his personal feelings get in the way of finishing the job he had come there to do—return Rain to her family.

So what was it? Was it just the cop in him, or maybe just the Navajo, he wasn't sure. But there was something about Logan Carvy—not Rain's husband, but about the man himself—that set his teeth on edge. Something he just didn't trust. Of course, the fact that Neal Rubin had told him that some of Carvy's business dealings and associates were questionable didn't help matters, either.

"Decent enough, I guess."

"You guess?"

He probably should have known he couldn't keep anything from Cruz. They'd been friends for too long; Cruz knew him too well not to read between the lines.

"I don't know," Joe confessed. "A little on the slick side, glib, cocky. It's just hard for me to imagine Rain with someone like him."

"Is that it? That all it is?"

Joe breathed out a silent laugh. Maybe Cruz had come to know him too well. "No, but it's not important whether I like the guy or not."

"Well, I don't envy you, friend," Cruz said in a quiet voice. "It's a tough position to be in."

He'd never talked with Cruz about his feelings for Rain—they were guys, they didn't talk feelings and emotions. They talked sports and politics and money. But they were also friends, friends who had seen each other through some pretty tough times and he didn't doubt for a moment that Cruz understood exactly how he felt about the woman and how difficult it would be to have to turn her over to another man—*any* other man.

"Call after the meeting tomorrow?"

"Will do," Joe promised.

He lowered the phone onto the cradle and fell back against the mattress. His body ached, his head pounded and his brain was exhausted. He wished he could just close his eyes and drift into the peaceful oblivion of sleep, but unfortunately he knew that wasn't going to happen. He'd been concerned that Rain hadn't gotten any rest in the last forty-eight hours, but the truth was he couldn't remember the last time he'd slept.

He closed his eyes, his mind playing a jumble of pictures, scrambled images and senseless sounds behind his lids. He thought back to the quiet nights they had spent in the loft of his cabin, of lying on the feather bed with Rain in his arms. Such peace he had known during those nights, a peace he couldn't even fathom now. It was if they had been in another time, another place, another galaxy.

Images of her flashed through his mind, frozen in time, trapped in his memory. Hundreds of scenes played through his brain like a slide show run amok— Rain laughing at a joke he'd told her, Rain working at her desk at the office, Rain wearing one of his T-shirts and nothing else, cooking eggs in the kitchen. Image after image, creating a portrait of what they had shared, a portrait of a woman dearly loved by her man.

He opened his eyes, staring up at the shadows streaking across the ceiling above the bed. Only he wasn't her man. Logan Carvy was her man.

Her man. The thought of Carvy with his beady blue eyes and thin lips that framed a mouth that turned up

on the ends in a perpetual smirk had a knot forming
in the pit of his belly. Was it that smirk that made him
uneasy, or was it something in the man's cold blue
gaze that brought the hair on the back of his neck
standing on end?

He thought of how Logan had acted, pompous and
insolent, but it was the way he talked that had sent
alarms going off in his head. The cocky way he'd answered their questions, flippant and insincere—like a
defendant on the stand lying through his teeth.

Lying. Joe turned and walked back to the bed. There
was nothing to indicate Carvy had been lying, nothing
other than his own suspicions, his own uneasiness. The
only one he knew for sure had been lying was himself.

Rain had asked him if Logan had spoken of her, if
he had talked about finding her, about wanting her
back and he had lied to her. The truth was, Logan had
said very little about finding his wife. He'd talked
about the kidnapping, about the ransom demands and
about the ordeal he'd been through, but he'd said very
little about finding her, about having her back again.

Even after he'd given Rain's pictures to Carvy to
identify. His reaction hadn't been right. Carvy hadn't
acted like a man who'd just been given a wonderful
gift, like a man who had just found the wife he thought
had been lost to him forever.

Joe pulled off his T-shirt, letting it fall to the bed
and headed for the shower. He hadn't the heart to tell
Rain her husband had looked at her picture with about
as much emotion as if he'd been looking at the latest
model of luxury car—maybe even less. He'd lied, he'd
covered for Logan Carvy because Rain had enough to
deal with, and a cold, unfeeling bastard for a husband
wasn't what she needed right now.

The hot water scaled his skin, but he steeled himself against it. He wanted to burn out all those unpleasant images, wanted the steam to sweat out all his suspicions and misgivings.

How was he going to do it? How was he going to walk away and leave her with that man? It would have been hard under any circumstances, even if he was returning her to a man who at least acted as though he were happy that she was found, but to someone like Carvy who had displayed no emotion at all— How was he going to do it?

He thought of Carvy again, about him touching Rain with his soft, fat fingers, about him embracing her with his short, thick arms. He thought of those thin lips kissing her warm mouth, thought of those cold, watery eyes looking at her beautiful body.

"No, no," he groaned in coarse, raw voice that echoed off the white tiled walls of the shower. "I—I can't. I can't do this. I can't."

But he had to. Somehow, some way he was going to have to find a way to do just that—to walk away, to stay away, to forget.

"No," he said again, his fist hitting the tile. "No."

Yanking the shower curtain to one side, he stalked out of the shower, out of the bathroom and to the telephone.

"Hello?"

FBI Agent Neal Rubin's voice sounded hoarse with sleep over the line.

"This is Joe Mountain," he announced, the carpet beneath his feet becoming soaked. "Tell me what you know about this Logan Carvy. I want to know everything."

Chapter 14

"You okay?"

The wave of nausea that washed over her was so strong it brought her to a dead stop. "I think I'm going to be sick."

Joe reached for her, catching her before her knees buckled beneath her.

"Maybe we should reschedule this."

"No!" She pushed him away and struggled to regain her balance. She pulled a deep, cleansing breath into her lungs. "I couldn't take it. Not another night like last night." She looked up at him, taking another deep breath. "Not again."

"I take it you didn't get any sleep."

"Not a wink," she confessed. She squinted, pointing to his bloodshot eyes. "You didn't fare much better."

"I look that bad?"

"No, you just look like someone who hasn't slept in two days." She straightened up, rubbing a hand over her volatile stomach and squared her shoulders. "But then, maybe it's just the suit. I've never seen you in one before."

Joe reached up and straightened his necktie. "Well if it makes me look like an insomniac, I may never wear one again."

Despite her ailing stomach, she had to smile. Actually, he looked so handsome in the dark-blue suit with his long hair pulled back into a long ponytail, it almost hurt too much to look at him. But she had resigned herself to what was happening, resigned herself to her fate.

Somewhere in the night she'd trembled all she was going to, worried all she could. It was as if she had exhausted all her fears, all her nerves, all her anxieties. She would never find peace with the situation, but somewhere in the night she'd found an acceptance. Like a prisoner facing the gallows, she had accepted the inevitable. She just hoped she could do it without throwing up.

"The funny thing is," she said, trying not to think too much about just how handsome he did look, "I don't feel tired."

"No?"

They both turned at the sound of the elevator.

"No, too much adrenaline I guess." She started for the empty elevator, motioning for him to follow. "Come on, let's get this over with."

"You sure you're up to it?" he asked, reaching out to hold the elevator door for her. "I mean, if you need a little more time—an hour or two to get ready—"

"I'm fine," she said, straightening her jacket. She'd labored a good part of the morning trying to decide what to wear for this first meeting, finally deciding on a sedate wool blazer with a matching knee-length skirt. She had never worn the suit. It had been part of the wardrobe she had bought on her shopping spree with Marcy.

She remembered how delighted they had been that she'd gotten it on sale, and how she had saved it in her closet for a special occasion.

She ran a hand over her skirt, smoothing out the fabric. She sort of thought the "special occasion" would be a dinner out with Joe or something like that—not the day she would be forced to say goodbye to him.

He stepped into the elevator behind her and the door silently closed behind him. He pushed the button for the lobby and they both stood there, watching the numbers of the floor tick by, one after the other.

She was still reeling from the sudden recollection last night, remembering Christian and Robyn, but so many parts of the puzzle remained missing. She had no recollection of giving birth to them, no recollection of the common, ordinary, everyday mothering of them. And probably most disturbing of all, she had no recollection of who their natural father was. All she knew was that Logan Carvy was their stepfather.

But she did remember the love. Despite all the gaps in her memory, she knew without a doubt that she loved Christian and Robyn and somehow, that made today just a little bit easier.

"Are we taking a cab?"

"No. Actually, an FBI agent is meeting us downstairs. An Agent Rubin."

She watched the buttons light up, counting down fourteen, thirteen, twelve. "FBI? Is that necessary?"

"Just procedure," he said, watching the buttons,

too. "Unlike missing persons, kidnapping is a federal offense. Technically this is still their case."

"But, you'll be coming with us, right?"

"Of course."

The buttons continued to light, one after the other, the motion of the elevator making her feel light-headed.

"Joe," she said, watching as the buttons six, five and four lit up.

"Yes?"

Three. Two.

"I love you."

He turned his head, looking at her as the bell rang for the lobby. "I know."

The doors slid open and she stepped off the elevator. She didn't want to look at him—she couldn't, or she probably never would have been able to go through with all this.

It really hadn't been necessary for her to tell him how she felt. He already knew. But she'd just wanted to say it again, wanted to say it one last time while she was still Rain, before they stepped off the elevator and went their separate ways. She just wanted to hear the words one more time because she would be feeling them in her heart for the rest of her life.

"Sheriff Mountain."

Rain hadn't needed anyone to tell her who the middle-aged man with the crew cut and dressed in a dark-gray suit was. He looked just exactly what she had imagined an FBI agent would look.

"Agent Rubin," Joe said formally, extending his hand. "Neal, this is…well, this is the woman you came to meet."

"Ma'am," Rubin said politely. "I know Sheriff

Mountain has explained to you we've arranged a meeting at the Carvy house this morning.''

"Yes, he has," she said, feeling a little as though the floor beneath her feet was still descending at a rapid rate.

"Sheriff Mountain thought you'd be more comfortable if this first interview took place at the Carvy residence."

"Interview?" She stopped as they started for the door.

"You've been the victim of a federal crime," Rubin explained. "We'd like the opportunity to ask you about that."

"You realize I don't remember a lot."

Rubin glanced up at Joe, then back to her. "The sheriff has explained your injuries." He motioned toward the door again. "And as you probably already know, your husband identified you last night from the photographs the sheriff brought, but the meeting this morning will just make it official."

"Official," she mumbled as she let the two men escort her out of the hotel and into the unmarked sedan that was waiting.

"You doing okay?" Joe asked, ducking his head inside before closing the car door.

There was such emotion on his face, such feeling in his eyes. He had never told her he loved her, had never said what he felt for her or what their time together had meant to him. Maybe he didn't love her, maybe he'd been motivated more by pity than by any true feelings for her, but she had touched something in him. It was there on his face and in his eyes. He would go back to Mesa Ridge, back to his job, to his ranch and in time he'd forget about her. But she would never forget him. They would be thousands of miles apart, but Joe Mountain was going to be with her always.

"I'm fine," she whispered, settling into the back seat and reaching for the seat belt.

He hesitated for a moment, then straightened up and slammed the door closed.

"It's about a twenty-minute drive to the house," Rubin said, peering at her from the driver's seat through the rearview mirror. He twisted the key in the ignition, bringing the engine to life. "Traffic should be pretty light this time of day."

Joe slipped into the front passenger seat across from Rubin and adjusted the seat belt. "We're in no hurry." He turned to Rain in the back seat. "Are we?"

She didn't answer, she couldn't. She was afraid if she opened her mouth she would either start screaming, or throw up—neither of which she wanted to do. So she just kept her mouth shut and turned her head. She looked out the window, watching the buildings pass in a blur. The city had a cold, unfamiliar feel to it. It didn't feel like home, didn't feel warm or welcoming. Would it ever? Would she ever feel as though she belonged, or would she always feel like a stranger?

She thought of Christian and Robyn. Her children. She remembered them, loved them—loved them dearly. The love was there in her heart, real and sincere. She wanted to see them, to gather them into her arms and hold and nurture them. So why didn't she feel like a mother, why didn't she feel like *their* mother?

She looked at Joe, sitting in the seat. Was it always going to be this way? Was there always going to be gaps in her memory, pieces missing from her life? She was a mother who couldn't remember what it was like to be a mother. She was a wife who couldn't remember her husband but remembered all too well the love she felt for another man.

This was more than just her homecoming. This was her moment of truth, her Armageddon, her Waterloo.

She watched as they left the skyscrapers and the office buildings behind and the landscape became more suburban. But as warm and comfortable the parks and the homes looked, nothing looked familiar.

"The Carvy house is just ahead," Rubin announced, looking at her through the rearview mirror again.

Rain leaned forward, glancing out the front window. The homes had become mansions, but catching sight of a large Tudor-style home peeking out from atop a tree-lined drive had something flashing in her memory. She didn't need the FBI agent to tell her which house belonged to Logan Carvy. She already knew which one it was. She had been there before, had driven up that drive, had been inside that house.

"Rain," Joe asked, reaching for her from the front seat. "What is it? What's the matter?"

Staring at the house, she pointed. "That's it. That's the one right there." She shifted her gaze, looking at him. "I've been here before. I—I remember."

"She's right," Rubin affirmed.

Joe's gaze bounced to the agent, then back to her. Finding her hand, he squeezed it tight. "Are you okay? Do you want to stop for a while?"

But she couldn't answer, couldn't speak. She could only sit there and shake her head. Something was happening. She knew it, could feel it.

She sank back against the seat, closing her eyes to the disjointed images that flashed through her mind. It was almost there, she could almost touch it, almost remember.

"Rain, look at me," Joe demanded. "Open your eyes. Rain, please."

"Joe," she groaned, watching the pictures in her brain. What was it she was seeing? Who were those people? Where was that place? She opened her eyes, turning to him. "Joe. I've been here before. I know it...I remember."

"Pull the car over," he ordered Rubin.

Her heart was pounding by the time Agent Rubin brought the car to a stop at the curb.

Joe was out of the car and by her side before she had a chance to open her eyes.

"Rain, talk to me," he pleaded, taking her hand. "Are you all right?"

She opened her eyes, gazing up at him. It had been so close, so close she'd almost been able to touch it. Except her fingers had only been able to brush the surface; she hadn't been able to grasp hold, hadn't been able to pull it back.

"I'm okay," she assured him. His face was streaked with worry and she felt her heart pound even harder. "I thought for a moment..." She stopped and shook her head. How could she explain to him what she didn't understand herself? "I'm fine now. Just let me catch my breath."

"Rubin, turn the car around. We'll reschedule for later—"

"No," she insisted, shaking her head. She turned to him, slipping her palm along his cheek. He was such a good man, was capable of such warmth, such caring. This was as difficult for him as it was for her, and the last thing she wanted was to prolong the agony for either of them. "We've come this far."

"But if it's this hard on you—"

"It's just nerves," she lied. She dropped her hand and sat up. "And I'm feeling much better now."

He looked less than convinced, but as though sensing her determination, he slid out of the car and into the front seat again.

They were all quiet as Rubin drove the standard-issue government sedan through the open iron gates of the Carvy home and up the shady drive. When he brought the car to a stop in the center of the circular drive, she opened the door and stepped out onto the drive on her own.

There was something happening inside her. She knew it just as she knew the sun would set in the west and rise tomorrow in the east. She couldn't explain it, didn't even want to talk about it, but she knew Logan Carvy held the key to everything.

She wanted to meet the man, wanted to see the person who was her husband—not because he had identified her as his wife, not because she thought she loved him and not even because it was the right thing to do.

For weeks she had been living on the edge of a black hole not knowing where she had come from or where she was going and too frightened to think about either. But she wasn't afraid anymore. From the moment she had walked out of the desert and into Joe Mountain's arms, her entire life rotated around Logan. He had been there from the beginning—first in her dreams and now in her reality. Logan had bridged the gap between the past and the present, had remained the only constant in a life of chaos and question. It was as if she had died and had been reborn and somehow it all revolved around Logan.

She looked up at the house Logan Carvy called home, the house she could almost remember, the house he had shared with his wife. No, she wasn't afraid, she was determined. She wanted this to happen, insisted that it happen. She'd had her fill of questions with no answers, had enough of being afraid and not knowing why. This was the day of reckoning, the day all her questions were answered and all the dark spots in her life thrown into the light.

"Ready?" Joe asked, walking around the car to her.

She looked up, feeling more certain, more confident than she had in her life. "Let's do it."

Something changed the moment she walked through Logan Carvy's house. It was as if she had transformed before his eyes. She didn't have to say anything, didn't have to tell him or even open her mouth—it was written all over her face. He had been walking beside her when she'd stepped inside the house, when the past ascended from the ashes like a phoenix rising and hit her right between the eyes.

A housemaid was escorting them through the foyer and into the living room, but he was barely aware of it. His entire focus was on Rain and what was happening to her.

Since his midnight call to Neal Rubin, his apprehension about this morning had grown. He wasn't sure if he felt vindicated or just more disturbed when he learned Logan Carvy had succeeded in raising the suspicions of the FBI, as well. According to Rubin, they had questioned Carvy's delay in reporting his wife's kidnapping and had found that suspicious from the beginning. Of course, they both had to admit that there was no hard evidence to show that Carvy was anything other than what he appeared, but as seasoned lawmen, they'd both learned to rely on their instincts and instincts were telling them Carvy was hiding something.

Of course, all this only made this morning's meeting all the more impossible for him. Leaving Rain with a husband she didn't remember was difficult enough. Leaving her with a man who couldn't be trusted was damn near impossible. His reservation had him leaving for Nevada tonight, but he wasn't sure he'd be able to get on that plane—at least until he figured out just what Logan Carvy was hiding.

Her hand on his arm scattered his troubled thoughts and brought him to an abrupt halt.

"I need to sit down," she mumbled in a whisper.

She looked deathly white and her half-closed eyes looked glassy and unable to focus.

"Right, right," he said, banking down the panic he felt. Rushing, he all but carried her around a gaudy, high-backed embroidered sofa that stood facing away from the living room entrance. Settling her on an unyielding cushion, he knelt in front of her.

"I think maybe we should call a doctor," he said, glancing up at Agent Rubin.

"No!" she insisted, blindly clutching at him.

"Rain, you're sick," he said turning back to her. "You need help—"

"It's…it's coming back," she whispered. "Joe, it's coming back."

"Gentlemen."

Joe glanced up and peered over the back of the sofa as Logan Carvy walked into the room.

"Agent Rubin," he said with a curt nod. "Sheriff...Mountain, was it? Have you brought my wife?"

"Mr. Carvy," Neal Rubin began, pulling a cell phone from his pocket. "I'm afraid the lady isn't feeling well—"

"What do you mean she's not feeling well?" Carvy demanded, moving forward. "Rachel, are you sick?"

"Logan."

In a startling moment, Rain was suddenly on her feet and facing the man who was her husband.

"Darling, it's me," Carvy said, walking around the sofa. "It's Logan, your husband."

"You're not my husband," Rain announced, bringing Carvy to a dead stop.

She wasn't pale any longer and her eyes were wide and clear with confidence—and knowledge.

"He's not my husband," she repeated, turning to Joe.

"Rachel darling, what are you saying?" Carvy insisted with a nervous laugh, looking to Agent Rubin and then to Joe. "Gentlemen, I understand what you mean. It's obvious my wife is very ill."

"I am not your wife," Rain announced in a steady voice, taking several challenging steps toward Carvy. "But I know who you are and I know what you've done." She didn't stop until she was practically nose to nose with the man. "You see, Logan, I remember. I remember everything."

Chapter 15

"Carly."

She folded the old football jersey she used as a nightshirt and nodded. "That's right. Carly Davis of Lake Tahoe, California, teacher at Vina Danks Junior High at your service."

She packed the shirt into the suitcase and reached for her hairbrush and makeup bag. The name sounded right to her, comfortable and familiar like an old friend too long absent.

"That's a lot to remember and is going to take some getting used to." Joe leaned back in the chair and watched as she gathered up the rest of her possessions and slipped them into the suitcase. He was in his sheriff's uniform again, but his necktie hung loose and the top button on his shirt fell open. "Is it feeling right to you yet?"

She stopped and thought for a moment. It was all she could do to keep her composure, to keep herself from stalking over to him and demanding to know what he thought he was doing. How could he just sit there chatting with her after what had happened?

"Yeah, it is," she said turning to him. "But not as right as Rain."

He looked at her and she looked at him, but neither one of them laughed at the bad pun.

"What time is your flight to Denver?"

"Eleven-forty-five." She glanced down at her wrist watch. Was he anxious to get rid of her? "I've got about an hour yet."

"Christian and Robyn know you're coming?"

She had to smile, remembering their voices on the phone. "Yes, and I've talked to their grandparents. I've told them what happened and they want to wait until I get there to say anything to the children."

"They'll need you now."

"We'll need each other to get through this," she sighed. "What about you? When are you heading back?"

"I'm taking a red-eye out tonight. Ryan's putting together a team right now but I want to be there in the morning when they start the search."

She squeezed her eyes tight, the nightmare alive in her memory now. "You'll let me know, when you find...when you find the body?"

"Of course," he assured her quietly. "Were you able to get any rest last night?"

"My adrenaline level was a little high—and of course Marcy and I were on the phone for almost two hours, but yeah, I slept." She closed her suitcase, wanting to talk about something else, wanting to get her mind off the desert and a scene so horrible she didn't want to remember. "How about you? How late did you stay at the FBI headquarters?"

"It was late," he confessed. "Carvy had to be booked and fingerprinted, and he couldn't be interviewed until after his lawyer got there."

Rain stopped as she zipped her suitcase closed. Why hadn't he come to her room last night? Why had he let her spend the night alone?

"It's still so hard to believe," she said, walking to the window and gazing out. "Did all that happen just yesterday?"

"What a difference a day makes," Joe said, rising to his feet.

She turned around, staring at him from across the room. "There isn't any chance...I mean, a judge wouldn't let him out on bail or anything like that?"

"Don't worry. Logan Carvy isn't going anywhere for a very long time."

She would have felt much better, more assured if he would just walk across the room and put his arms around her, but he didn't.

This was the first time they'd been alone since... since what? Her revelation? Her rebirth? Since her past came out of the darkness and smacked her right between the eyes?

To say she'd been on an emotional roller coaster would be the understatement of all time. She'd not only been put through the wringer, she'd been to hell and back again as well.

She rejoiced in recovering her past, rejoiced in knowing once and for all who she was, but the discovery had come with a price. She'd awakened to disturbing memories and a loss she'd never truly recover from.

Rachel Carvy—wife of Logan, mother of Christian and Robyn...and sister to Carly Davis. Rachel Logan had never been kidnapped, she'd been hunted, the prey of a deadly predator who wanted her at all costs.

Rachel hadn't known who Logan Carvy was when she'd married him. Widowed and struggling to raise her two children on her own, Rachel had thought she'd finally met the man of her dreams when she'd met Logan, thought he would give her and her children the kind of stable, loving home they needed.

It wasn't until after the wedding that Rachel had discovered her new husband's seedy underside, his violent temper, his questionable business practices and his connection to organized crime. It had taken her nearly five years to work up the courage to walk out on the abusive relationship, but when she had, she'd run to her sister for help.

But Carvy wasn't about to sit by and watch his wife walk out on him. Determined to get her back, he had dispensed two goons to find her and bring her back.

Rain closed her eyes, remembering the night she'd opened her front door to find a terrified Rachel standing there. Having sent her children to their paternal grandparents in Denver for safekeeping, Rachel had pleaded for her help, but Rain hadn't gotten the chance to help her sister. Carvy's henchmen had found them, chasing them down, threatening them with guns and taking them both captive.

It had been a brave and foolish thing Rachel had done, trying to divert their attention by making a run for it and she had paid dearly for her act. It had been a black night, dark clouds having covered the moon and heavy winds whipping through the desert canyons.

The spot they had chosen to stop at had seemed so cold and forbidding.

The men must have known what would happen to them if they were to have touched the wife of Logan Carvy, which was why they had gone after Rain. She could still smell the vile breath of the drunken bastards who had tried to touch her, still see the cruel intent in their eyes.

Unable to sit by and watch her sister be assaulted, Rachel had started out across the desert in an effort to divert their attention, in an effort to save her sister and unfortunately it had worked. Rain would have greatly preferred the loathsome attack to what resulted from Rachel's noble gesture.

When Rachel took off, the men had jumped into the car and taken off after her. Whether it had been their intent to hit Rachel, or just give her a scare, would never to clear. But intentional or not, they struck her with the hood of the car, killing her instantly.

They must have panicked then, having lost all amorous intentions. The last thing Rain remembered before the blinding pain at the back of her head had been screaming Logan's name. Logan Carvy had been responsible for this. He had killed Rachel just as surely as if he'd been sitting behind the wheel of that car and run her down himself. He'd taken her sister's life and left her in the desert for dead—and now it was time he paid.

''I'll have to come back for their trial, no doubt?''

Joe nodded. ''No doubt, but that won't be for months now.''

''Well, I guess that's it,'' she said, looking around the room. ''I think I've got everything.''

''I'll take you to the airport.''

"That's not necessary," she insisted. "I can get a cab."

"Don't be silly," he said, waving off her suggestion. "I'll get your bag."

"No, really," she insisted, as he grabbed the bag off the bed and started for the door. "I don't want to put you to any trouble."

"No trouble," he said, opening the door and holding it for her.

She started through the door, then came to an abrupt halt. "No, I take that back."

He hesitated for a moment, confused. "What?"

"I take that back," she said again, her hands going stubbornly to her hips.

"You take what back?"

"I want to make some trouble."

He stepped back inside the room, letting the door swing closed behind him. "Rain—er, Carly, what are you talking about?"

"You," she said, pointing an accusing finger. "I can't believe you. You make me so mad."

"Mad? What did I do?"

"You were going to do it, weren't you? You were going to stand right there and do it."

"Do what? Rain—I mean—" He set the suitcase down. "Damn it, Rain, Carly, whatever the hell your name is. I don't know what you're talking about. What did I do?"

"Do?" she said, her voice almost a shriek. "You didn't *do* anything, that's just it. You were going to stand there and let me walk out of your life and *do* nothing to stop me!"

"No, I wasn't."

"Oh, yes, you were," she insisted. "I'm all packed,

my plane takes off in less than an hour and there you are, carrying my suitcase to the car.'' She stalked up to him. "What's the matter with you? Don't you care about me at all?"

"Rain—"

"After all, I know now that I'm not married, I don't have anyone special in my life, there's no reason in the world we shouldn't be able to keep seeing one another and yet you're going to just let me go."

"Carly, stop."

"You haven't so much as touched me since you learned the truth, Joe. What's the matter? What are you afraid of?"

"Afraid?" He pushed past her, pacing across the room and back again. "Did it ever occur to you that you may need some time to get your life together, to see how you feel, to see what you want?"

"You don't think I know what I want."

"I think you've been through a lot," he said, pacing again. "You finally get your memory back only to remember seeing your sister murdered. You don't think that might cloud your judgment? You don't think it might change the way you feel?"

"Maybe it's not me you're concerned about changing," she pointed out, reaching out and stopping his pacing. "Maybe you're the one who's changed. I'm not an enigma anymore, not a woman of mystery. You found out I wasn't anyone glamorous or famous, I'm just plain old Carly—an ordinary schoolteacher who lives by herself and likes to bird watch and cook lavish meals in her spare time. There's nothing too exciting about that, is there, Joe? Nothing much to hold a man's interest."

"Is that what you think?" he demanded. "The mystery is solved so I'm not interested anymore?"

Emotion clutched at her throat, but her pride wouldn't let it show. "You tell me."

"You've got your life back," he said in a tightly controlled voice. "I thought you might need some time to…"

"To what?" she demanded, when his words drifted off.

He took a deep breath, turning away. He didn't look angry any longer, just defeated. "I thought you might need some time to see if you still needed me."

Her heart swelled into her throat. "Joe," she said, reaching out to him. "I told you I loved you and I meant it. Nothing—not Logan Carvy, not what happened, not even my old life is ever going to change that."

"Are you sure?"

She tried to pull him close, but he resisted. "Oh, Joe, don't you know? I've never been so sure about anything in my life."

He stopped struggling then and pulled her into his arms. "Rain. Carly."

"Your Rain," she murmured. "Your Carly."

His kiss was hard but not brutal and she felt whole for the first time in her life.

"I love you," he whispered. "Always and forever."

"I love you, too."

"Think you can handle another name change?"

"Rain and Carly aren't enough for you?"

"They're fine for the first names. I was thinking of working on last names this time."

She could barely hear for the thunder of her heart. "Oh?"

"Marry me?"

"When? Where?"

"Whenever you want, wherever you say."

"I love you, Joe Mountain, and I'd love very much to be your wife."

"Promise?"

"Promise."

"Come on," he said, setting her away from him and reaching for her suitcase. "Help me pack. I'm going to Colorado with you. We'll make wedding plans on the way."

"Whatever you say. You're the sheriff."

*   *   *   *   *

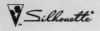

INTIMATE MOMENTS™

and

BEVERLY BARTON

present:

Ready to lay their lives on the line, but unprepared for the power of love

Available in March 2001:
NAVAJO'S WOMAN
(Intimate Moments #1063)
Heroic Joe Ornelas will do anything to shelter the woman he has always loved.

Available in May 2001:
WHITELAW'S WEDDING
(Intimate Moments #1075)
Handsome Hunter Whitelaw is about to fall in love with the pretend wife he only "wed" to protect!

And coming in June 2001, a brand-new, longer-length single title:
**THE PROTECTORS:
SWEET CAROLINE'S KEEPER**

Sexy David Wolfe longs to claim the woman he has guarded all his life—despite the possible consequences....

Available at your favorite retail outlet.

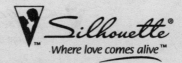

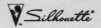

INTIMATE MOMENTS™

presents a riveting 12-book continuity series:

A Year of Loving dangerously

Where passion rules and nothing is what it seems...

When dishonor threatens a top-secret agency, the brave
men and women of SPEAR are prepared to risk it all as they
put their lives—and their hearts—on the line.

Available March 2001:

THE ENEMY'S DAUGHTER
by Linda Turner

When undercover SPEAR agent Russell Devane arrived at the
Pear Tree cattle station deep in the Australian outback, he had every
intention of getting close to the enemy's daughter. But all the rules
changed when Russell found himself fighting a forbidden attraction
to the breathtakingly beautiful Lise. Would he be able to capture
an evil traitor without forfeiting the love of a lifetime?

*Available only from Silhouette Intimate Moments
at your favorite retail outlet.*

Where love comes alive™

LINDSAY McKENNA

continues her most popular series with a
brand-new, longer-length book.

And it's the story you've been waiting for....

Morgan's Mercenaries:
Heart of Stone

They had met before. Battled before. And
Captain Maya Stevenson had never again
wanted to lay eyes on Major Dane York—
the man who once tried to destroy
her military career! But on their latest
mission together, Maya discovered that beneath
the fury in Dane's eyes lay a raging passion. Now she
struggled against dangerous desire, as Dane's command
over her seemed greater still. For this time, he laid claim
to her heart....

Only from Lindsay McKenna and Silhouette Books!

> "When it comes to action and romance,
> nobody does it better than Ms. McKenna."
> —*Romantic Times Magazine*

Available in March at your favorite retail outlet.

Silhouette®
Where love comes alive™

PSMMHOS

HARLEQUIN®

bestselling authors

Merline Lovelace
Deborah Simmons
Julia Justiss

cordially invite you to enjoy three brand-new stories of unexpected love

The Officer's Bride

Available April 2001

HARLEQUIN®

Makes any time special ®

Every mother wants to see her children marry
and have little ones of their own.

One mother decided to take matters into
her own hands....

Now three Texas-born brothers are about to discover
that mother knows best: A strong man *does* need a
good woman. And babies make a forever family!

Matters of the Heart

A Mother's Day collection of
three **brand-new** stories by

Pamela Morsi
Ann Major
Annette Broadrick

Available in April at your favorite retail outlets,
only from Silhouette Books!

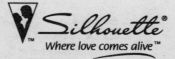

Where love comes alive™